EDGE:
ASHES AND DUST

Edge:
Ashes and Dust

GEORGE G. GILMAN

NEW ENGLISH LIBRARY
TIMES MIRROR

A New English Library Original Publication, 1976
© 1976 by George G. Gilman

*

FIRST NEL PAPERBACK EDITION MAY 1976

*

NEL Books are published by
New English Library Limited from Barnard's Inn, Holborn, London, E.C.1.
Made and printed in Great Britain by Hunt Barnard Printing Ltd., Aylesbury, Bucks.

45002813 5

for
S.M.
who spreads the word while
I stay out of the picture.

Chapter One

THE glass-sided hearse was drawn by two black horses, and four men rode in escorting positions, two on each flank. The progress of the small funeral procession was appropriately slow but it nonetheless moved in a pall of red Texas dust formed by a fusion of the many minor explosions of motes from beneath plodding hooves and turning wheel rims.

Thus, an interested observer would have difficulty in picking out individual details of the hearse, the two living passengers it carried and the quartet of riders surrounding it.

But the sole observer was totally indifferent to this first sign of life – and death – he had seen in many days. Sitting on his bedroll in the mouth of a cave, shaded from the harsh glare of the early morning sun, he continued with the chore of shaving. He had no mirror to foreshorten the focus of his eyes and he looked at the hearse and escort simply because they were in the centre of his field of vision.

He knew precisely where the horses would be reined to a halt, for the grave was ready dug. He had seen it the previous night, when he decided the cave-pocked hillside on the north bank of the Rio Grande provided a good place to bed down. Fresh dug, for the sandy soil displaced from the deep, six feet by three hole was damp. He had been mildly intrigued, but no more than this.

Now, as the dust settled on and around the stalled hearse and horses, his mind registered the scene and its component movements with a complete lack of emotion. He was as detached and unfeeling as the rocky hill slope from which he watched.

The Rio Grande was better than a hundred and fifty feet wide at this point, flowing muddily between low, sparsely vegetated banks. Behind the northern bank were the foothills of the Texan Santiago Mountains. To the south was spread the arid ruggedness of the Sierra del Burro of Mexico's Coahuila region. Only the river drew a distinction between the two countries. The barren terrain was the same and the sun was as searingly cruel on both sides of the frontier.

'You dug the hole all by yourself, Miss Diamond? A lady like you?'

The speaker was one of the four horsemen. They had all dismounted and allowed their animals freedom to sidle across to the river's edge and drink: while they themselves went to the brink of the grave and peered down into its depths.

'I'll allow it was not an easy thing to do.'

The four dismounted men were like the country surrounding them. Big, rugged and covered with red dust. They looked like cowhands who had wandered in from the range without being entirely sure where or why they were going. And now that they were here they looked out of place and embarrassed. If they were mourners, they had not dressed for the part. They wore workaday denim pants and shirts and low-crowned, wide-brimmed hats. Each carried a holstered gun at his hip. Dust was clogged in their pores, held there by old sweat.

The woman seated beside the driver of the hearse looked even more out of keeping with the hot, harsh, empty Big Bend country of southern Texas. She was a tall, slender blonde in her late twenties or early thirties dressed entirely in black – shoes, ankle-to-throat loose-fitting gown, gloves and narrow-brimmed bonnet with a face-curtaining veil.

As she responded to the cowhand's comment, she raised the veil and brushed a white handkerchief over her face. The action revealed features that were both strong and handsome: could perhaps have been made beautiful by the skilful application of make-up. But the pale, blemish-free skin was untouched by paint or powder. And, looking across and down over a distance of some two hundred yards, the watcher in the cave was unable to catch more than a fleeting impression of possible beauty before the veil swung back to conceal the face.

'There really was no necessity, ma'am,' the driver of the hearse said as he carefully climbed down and then held out both hands to assist the woman.

He was a short, pot-bellied man of about sixty with a round, red face and bow-legs. He wore the black cassock and white reversed collar of a priest.

'It was necessary for me, Father Donovan,' the woman replied shortly as she allowed herself to be helped to the ground.

Their voices were carried a long way in the empty silence of the Big Bend country: the only other sounds the trickling of the sluggish river and the wheezy breathing of the weary horses. From the panting of the animals and the contoured lines of dust-coloured lather on their backs, it was obvious the funereal approach to the graveside had not been maintained from the procession's starting point. The pace had been fast and furious until the end was near.

'Shall we proceed?' the woman said after she had made a slow, complete about-turn. It was as if the grave she had dug was not sufficient by itself. Before the final act of the funeral took place, she wanted to assure herself that this section of riverside was the right one. And there were confirming landmarks – the western end of a butte at the top of the cave-riddled slope, which lined up with a distant pass between twin peaks in the Sierra del Burro.

'Whatever you say, Miss Diamond,' the eldest of the cowhands allowed. He tipped his hat off his head to hang down his back by the neck cord.

The others did likewise and then all four ambled self-consciously to the rear of the hearse. The priest reached up on to the seat and lifted down a heavy prayer-book. The woman moved to the side of the grave, opposite to where the displaced earth was heaped. She bowed her head and clasped her hands together on the shallow swell of her belly. Her back was towards the man in the cave as he finished shaving and tipped away the scummy water from the skillet.

He went to the rear of the cave, unfastened the hobble rope from his gelding's forelegs and led the animal forward. As he saddled him, the horse viewed the scene below with the same brand of disinterest as the man.

Although they were not dressed for their parts, the cowhands adopted suitably mournful expressions as they became pall-bearers. And their gait was measured as, with the plain pine box balanced on their broad shoulders, they moved from the hearse to the grave. The woman had to take two steps backwards to allow the men to get into position. The priest was already in his place at the head of the grave, the prayer-book open across his pudgy hands.

The woman nodded to the priest, who leaned close to the book to read from it with short-sighted eyes.

'We beseech you, O Lord to accept unto the Kingdom of Heaven the soul of this our departed brother, Boyce Robert Diamond. In common with all mortal men, he has sinned and . . .'

Father Donovan spoke with a rich, Irish brogue and as he intoned the prayers of the interment service his words rang across the empty country with a deep resonance. And, as if in deference to his sombre tones, the horses became quiet and even the river's gentle sounds seemed muted.

Up in the cave, the man adjusted the gelding's saddle cinch and began to pack his gear into the bedroll.

By pre-arrangement, or perhaps because of the mounting heat, the funeral service was short. The pallbearers lowered the casket into the grave. The four ropes were tied to each corner and when the box could sink no further they were released to thump hollowly on the pine lid.

'Ashes to ashes, dust to dust,' the priest intoned.

He closed his prayer book and in the silence that followed his final word the flat sound had the quality of a gunshot. The woman was first to stoop and scoop up a handful of dry dust. It floated rather than fell down into the grave. The four cowhands put their hats back on their heads before they made similar gestures to the corpse. There was another short interval of silence, then the woman swung away from the graveside and strode purposefully towards the hearse.

'Thank you for your assistance, gentleman,' she said, her voice as strong and as lacking in grief as before the service. 'I am most appreciative.'

'We can't say it was a pleasure, Miss Diamond,' the spokesman of the cowhands replied wetly, as if he felt the need to spit. 'But we're glad we could help a lady like you.'

There was a carpetbag on the running board of the hearse. The woman delved a gloved hand inside it and came up with four brown envelopes. 'Ten dollars per man,' she said. 'The agreed terms.'

Each man touched the brim of his hat as he accepted his envelope.

'Won't cost you no extra for me and the boys to fill in the grave, Miss Diamond.'

She shook her head. 'That will not be necessary. I wish you a pleasant ride back to Dream Creek, gentlemen.'

They all touched their hat brims again, and backed slowly away from the woman, like minions in the presence of an acknowledged better. Then they turned and their movements became hurried from the far side of the grave to where their horses waited. They mounted quickly, nodded their farewells to the priest, and heeled the animals into a canter. Dust from beneath the hooves drifted across the burial place and Father Donovan fanned a hand in front of his face. The woman was unconcerned by the swirling motes as she went to the still-open rear of the hearse and drew out a long-shafted shovel.

As she began to fill in the grave, the priest appeared set to

11

protest at a woman doing such work. But then he gave a shrug of resignation and moved to the hearse. He placed the prayer-book up on the seat, released the brake lever and led the two-horse team down to the edge of the river.

The animals sucked at the muddy water. The four riders crested a low rise and went from sight. The dust of their progress settled. The woman spaded dirt into the hole with a steady, seemingly effortless rhythm. The man in the cave checked that his gear was securely fastened, then swung up into the saddle. The gelding raised and turned his head to give the man a dispirited, one-eyed look.

'It's OK, feller,' the man muttered, stroking the horse's neck. 'Their mourning don't have to darken our day.'

He was about to urge the horse into movement with his un-spurred boot heels when a distant sound halted his action. It was a familiar enough sound, but one which he had not heard in many days – until the funeral procession had approached less than an hour previously. Now, others were nearing the lone grave. A lot faster than the hearse and its paid escort: and everyone riding a horse. No rig of any kind. At least half a dozen, riding animals with shod hooves.

They were coming from the west, riding around the base of the rise over which the four cowhands had gone from sight. The priest looked in that direction, peering anxiously across the downward canting necks of the drinking horses. The woman interrupted her work with the shovel and lifted her veil to gaze along the curve of the river bank. For no more than a second, the strength of her features was dissipated by naked terror. But then her jaw became firmly set and her mouthline registered defiance. The veil dropped back over her face as she stooped over the shovel and began to work frantically with it.

The man astride the horse in the cave sat and waited, as impassive as a carved statue. Until the silhouetted forms of six riders showed in the pall of their own dust, reining their mounts out of a gallop. Then he spat into the grey ashes of his doused fire.

'Texas is getting as overcrowded as hell has to be,' he rasped.

The grave was still less than three-quarters filled in when the

12

riders skidded their sweating mounts to a halt. For a few moments, as the dust drifted back to earth, they remained in a tight-knit group, midway between the hearse and the woman. The priest merely stood and looked, his once-red face suddenly a waxy white. The woman continued to work furiously with the shovel, ignoring the newcomers.

It was difficult to tell much about the six men. They were assorted shapes and sizes and wore dust-covered clothing bought for hard-wearing rather than style. The common denominator among them was that each had pulled up his neckerchief to conceal the lower half of his face.

'Don't keep on with the dirt spadin', lady. Only makin' extra work for us.'

'And we ain't ones for workin'!'

The first comment came from the biggest man in the bunch. Almost six inches over six feet, he had broad shoulders and barrel chest that swept down into his belly with no clearly defined waist line. The sleeves had been roughly torn out of his shirt and his burnished, hirsute arms seemed to have the colour and texture of strong young tree trunks. He spoke with a Southern drawl, pitched low.

The other speaker punctuated his remark with a musical laugh. High, like his voice, which also indicated his roots had been in the South. He was a head and shoulders shorter and his build was a lot slighter. His voice said he was several years younger.

' 'Ceptin' when it's worth our while, George.' This man was medium in all physical appearances – height, build and tone of voice. The kind of man who would not be noticed in a crowd. But he made himself noticed now, as the woman continued to pretend the men were not there. His right hand clawed out an Army Colt from a shoulder holster. Then he slowed his actions, to draw a bead at arm's length.

'Please don't!' the priest yelled.

The woman continued to remain inside the invisible shell of her private world. Until the gunshot and its bullet shattered the illusion. The bullet struck the shovel as she screamed: then ricochetted to bury itself in the diminished heap of dirt at the

13

graveside. The woman dropped the shovel as if the impact of the bullet had reverberated painfully up the wooden shaft.

'Con said to quit it, bitch!' the gunman rasped as he slid the gun back into its holster. Then he turned to glare at the priest, his eyes glinting out between the top of the mask and the shadow of his hat brim. 'And we don't want no more argument from you, holy man!'

'What do you want?' the woman demanded breathlessly. As she dropped the shovel, she had staggered backwards and gone into a half crouch to keep from toppling. Now she seemed frozen into the back-straining posture. It was obvious she was staring hard at the masked men from behind the veil.

'Reckon you know that,' the big man answered. 'And if you or the priest try to stop us puttin' our hands on it, this here place could get to be a regular little Boot Hill – you know what I mean?'

He carried a double-barrelled shotgun, slung to his back by a leather strap that was looped over his right shoulder and across his chest. The twin barrels were pointed downwards and the strap was loose. All he had to do was jerk on the leather and grab the gun at the frame and barrels as it swung around. He aimed it midway between the woman and the priest. His action was fast and the only accompanying sounds were the hiss of leather strap over denim shirt and the clicks of the cocking hammers.

'They quietened down all of a sudden, Con,' the youngster with the high-pitched voice said.

Con grunted, swung the gun and squeezed one of its triggers. The woman screamed again and fell hard to her rump. But she hadn't been hit. The charge had torn into the heap of dirt and sent a spray of it over the woman. The two horses hitched to the hearse had snorted when the revolver shot cracked out. At the louder blast, they reared. But they managed only a few strides of a potential bolt before the weight of the lock-wheeled hearse halted them. The horses of the masked men did not move a hoof. Neither did the mounted gelding in the cave.

'Reckon we can take it they know what I mean,' Con drawled. 'Get to it, boys.'

14

As the other five slid from their saddles and advanced on the grave, their leader broke his shotgun, ejected the spent cartridge and reloaded with a fresh one taken from a loop on his gunbelt.

'Opening a grave is sacrilege!' the priest exclaimed, his voice reedy with fear.

'Depends what it is a man worships, mister,' Con answered evenly. 'You and the woman just buried our Almighty.'

'I don't . . . I don't understand,' the priest stammered, eyes darting between the gun-toting man astride the horse and those at the grave.

The youngster had snatched up the shovel and dropped down into the hole. He started to hurl out showers of loose, dusty earth.

'Con means the Almighty dollar, holy man!' the one who had exploded his revolver yelled excitedly.

The priest continued to rake his confused gaze from Con to the graveside and back.

'It's my fault, Father!' the woman put in miserably, as she climbed painfully to her feet. 'I should have told you, but I didn't know – '

A short, very fat man took two fast paces towards the woman. His approach frightened the woman into silence and she raised her arms to defend herself. He laughed harshly, grasped one of her wrists and jerked it down and then up again. The woman shrieked her agony and was forced to turn around as the hammer lock was applied. The fat man's free hand streaked around her side and dodged her other hand. He cupped his palm and his blunt fingers clawed to fix an arrogant grip over the mound of her breast.

'Little missies like little children. Not speak unless spoken to.' He had the sing-song voice of an Oriental.

'Hold it, Jap!' Con yelled.

'Looks to me like that's what he's doin',' the man with the shoulder holster grunted.

'Ira?'

Con's tone of voice added a query to the name. Five of the masked men looked towards the sixth. He was almost as tall as Con, but carried a lot less weight. He was thin to the point of

15

near emaciation, so that his shoulder blades and ribs were contoured by the tight-fit of his red shirt. He tugged hard at his left earlobe, like a man immersed in deep, reflective thought.

'I come for my money, Con,' he responded at length. 'The Jap can have her if he's a mind.'

A low moan escaped from behind the woman's veil and her body, which had been rigid in the grasp of the Japanese, became abruptly limp. When he released her, she slumped to the ground as if in a faint.

The priest vented a louder moan and took a stride forward. The shotgun swung and exploded a second time. And the horses dragged the hearse another few yards. The ground immediately in front of the priest gave up countless spurts of dirt under the assault of the scattered charge. The priest froze.

Con laughed. 'You wait your turn, mister!' he taunted.

George, the youngster in the grave, was working furiously with the shovel again. The three men on the edge of the hole watched his efforts with eager concentration. The Jap went down on one knee beside the crumpled woman and hooked clawed fingers over the neckline of her mourning gown. His other hand fastened around her throat to hold her still as he jerked at the gown. The fabric ripped with the ease of damp paper, but with a more dramatic sound. But the stitching of the waistline refused to part. The Jap gave a grunt of displeasure.

'This bestiality must end!' the priest shrieked, and lunged into a waddling run.

The second trigger of the shotgun was squeezed. The range was less than fifteen feet and the moving target was sideways-on to the gunman. Father Donovan vented a groan that might have been pity for the woman or an expression of his agony. Then he froze in his tracks, remained standing for a moment, and finally toppled like a felled tree. The upper pattern of the shot tore the flesh from his face: the lower almost ripped off his arm. Blood and tiny pieces of tissue sprayed through hot air as he fell. As he became inert against the dusty ground, his mutilated side remained uppermost. Planes of white skull bone gleamed brilliantly through the bubbles of crimson. His left eye had dis-

16

integrated, but the gory cluster of nerves and pulp in the socket seemed to have the power to see and to express a tacit curse towards the priest's killer.

'For you, everythin's ended – you know what I mean?' Con growled, as he broke the smoking shotgun to eject the spent shells and reload.

Familiar with the reports which had not harmed them, the hearse team were calmer now. They merely flared their nostrils and bulged their eyes as they caught the scent of burnt powder and fresh blood. A swarm of flies zoomed in from under the river bank and settled to feast on the sheened crimson spilled by the shattered head and torso of the priest.

The woman moaned as the Jap flipped her over on to her belly with a hand and a foot and drew a knife. The man with the shoulder holster was the only one to glance away from the deepening grave to rake distasteful eyes over the corpse.

'I don't go for killin' holy men, Con,' he said flatly.

'That mean you don't go for me being top hand no more, Ken?' Con asked in the same tone.

Ken looked fleetingly at Con now, but with the light of humour in his eyes above the mask. 'But I guess I'll get over it.'

Con nodded. 'That's good, Ken. For you – you know what I mean?'

The Jap wrenched the torn dress off the woman's prone form and, where it held at the shoulders and waist, he used the knife. The blade glinted in the sunlight against the mourning black of the fabric. She remained totally limp and no more sounds escaped her mouth, which was pressed into the dust. Her attacker's breathing became as loud as the buzz of the flies, and he grunted in time with the thud of the shovel into the dirt as he worked on her underwear with the knife.

'Man!' he rasped as he turned her over on to her back again and snatched off her hat so that she was naked except for the sleeves of the dress and the gloves.

Ken shot a glance over his shoulder. His attention was distracted for longer this time, as his still-smiling eyes surveyed the body of the woman. The smooth whiteness of the skin contrasted vividly with the black of the fabric still clinging to her arms and hands: its starkness relieved only by the brown nipples cresting the small mounds of her breasts and the triangle of tangled, corn-coloured hair arrowing between her slim thighs.

'Nah, Jap!' Ken growled. 'You been without too long, I reckon. That there's a woman.'

He laughed and swung back towards the grave as George hit the casket lid with his shovel. The laugh became a yell of delight. George giggled and worked even faster at the digging. The man beside Ken dropped to his haunches. Con clucked his horse forward as he swung the shotgun round on to his back. Ira rubbed the palms of his hands together as if they itched.

'Nice, missy,' the Jap crooned, unfastening the front of his pants and rooting inside at his crotch. 'You like Japanese girl. No fight her man.'

Since she had been rolled on to her back to expose her most intimate parts to any who cared to look, the woman had been as inert as a corpse. But now, as the obese Jap parted her thighs into a broad vee and knelt between them, she expelled her pent up breath. And this triggered her creamy white flesh into a violent trembling motion. Which acted to arouse the Jap's lust to a greater pitch. So that his own exposed genitals swelled to the limit as he lowered himself down on to the quivering belly and breast.

The shovel was hitting the casket lid at every thrust now. Con and Ira watched in silence. George and the other two were yelling and laughing. Nobody at the grave heard the woman's shriek of pain as the Jap forced himself into an entry. His hands rose away from himself and formed into claws to fasten over the woman's breasts. She spread her arms as wide as her legs and wrenched her head to the side. Her eyes snapped open, staring but seeing nothing. Her lips moved, forming unspoken words. The Jap buried his masked face between her breasts as his hands rolled the firm flesh against his cheeks.

His back rose and fell, the thrusts of his panting lust taking their time from the cadence of the grave opening.

Up the hill, in the shaded mouth of the cave, the man astride the gelding took the makings from his shirt pocket and rolled a cigarette. He reached above him to strike the match on the cave roof, then drew deeply against the cigarette. His horse remained utterly still, preferring the illusion of coolness inside the cave to the undeniable high heat which shimmered out in the open. Blue cigarette smoke drifted outside, hovered for awhile, then rose suddenly upwards on an eddying thermal.

The Jap spent himself in a shuddering climax and became as limp as his victim.

George tossed out the ends of the four ropes and was hauled up from the grave. The casket was raised, the grunts of the sweating men competing with the hungry sounds of the feeding flies. Con leaned forward, to peer over the head of his horse. The Jap lifted himself out and off of the woman with a sigh. He picked up his discarded knife and replaced it in the belt sheath before he fastened his pants. Then he lifted the lower section of his bandana mask and spat on to the woman's belly.

'Missy need more practice,' he said, and swung towards the grave, where Ira had snatched up the shovel and was using it to lever off the lid of the dusty casket.

The spittle trickled down the woman's belly into the blood-soaked pubic triangle as her body heaved and vomit spewed from her gaping mouth. The flies swarmed from the dead man to the living woman.

Ira gave a final wrench with the shovel and the lid came free with a squeal of tortured wood and nails.

'Will you look at that!' George yelled, and his musical laughter masked the sound of the woman's retching.

The man in the cave showed a first flicker of interest, waving a hand to clear the tobacco smoke from in front of his face. He saw that only Ira had leaned over the open casket – to pick up a hessian-wrapped package. As Ira straightened, the Jap drew his knife again. The knife was offered, handle-first, and Ira took it after tugging once at his ear-lobe. The woman's nausea was finished and only the buzzing of the flies competed with the sound of the knife blade slicing through the hessian. When it had done its work, the fabric fell apart and all eyes except those of the now-silent woman drank in the sight of the pile of bills which was exposed.

'You sure didn't give us no bum steer, Ira,' Con growled.

George dragged his gaze away from the money to peer into the casket. There was no corpse to be seen – just twin rows of hessian-wrapped packages. 'There's gotta be a fortune here!' he yelled.

Con abruptly broke the spell which sight of the money had cast over him. He sat erect in the saddle and raked his gaze in every direction. But, if he had sensed the watcher in the hillside cave, he failed to spot the man.

'And there's gotta be a better place to count it – you know what I mean?' he snapped.

The men on the ground responded at once. Ken went to get the horses while the others hurried to lift the packages from the casket. There was just the single layer, beneath which was the waxed-faced, linen-clad corpse of a wizened old man.

As the bundles of money were packed into saddlebags, Con continued to survey the surrounding country. His body was rigid, his eyes unblinking, and he constantly fingered the strap of the shotgun. Once, he stared hard at one of the many cave mouths pocking the hillside to the north. He thought he saw a trace of smoke. But then he shook his head. Heat shimmer was everywhere, making a man's mind susceptible to mirages.

'All done, Con,' George reported, and the men swung up into their saddles, knees banging against bulging bags. 'What about Emma?'

For the first time since the opening of the new grave had commenced, all six men looked towards the woman: now as unmoving as the two corpses.

Then Con shrugged. 'Up to Ira, I reckon.'

The emaciated-looking man tugged at his mask so that it became free of his face and dropped into its more usual role as a neckerchief. With his features fully exposed, the impression of near-fleshless gauntness was strengthened.

'She won't cause no trouble,' he rasped with hate.

'Missy sure did not give me any!' the Jap growled as he and the others tugged off their masks. He laughed. 'I broke her real good, uh?'

'So let's move out!' Con barked across a peal of laughter from the other men.

He was the first to wheel his horse and thud in his spurred heels. The rest were quick to follow, and galloping hooves raised the inevitable cloud of red dust to shroud riders and mounts. Con looked back over his shoulder once, but the billowing pall made it difficult to see even the men immediately behind him. Thus, the scene of slaughter and rape at the river's side was totally veiled to him. Likewise, the man astride the gelding riding slowly down the hillside from the cave.

The lone rider halted his horse at the brink of the grave as the group of men rode out of sight around the hump of the hill from which they had first appeared. The sound of hoofbeats diminished and then ceased to vibrate the hot air. The buzzing of the flies took on a lazy quality as the scavengers neared the point of satiation.

The man astride the gelding looked down impassively at the violated body of the woman. The creamy whiteness of her flesh was now coated with settled dust, held there by sweat: and this sticky cloaking underplayed the bruises and small cuts caused by the Jap's lustful fingers and nails. The stench of her drying vomit was stronger than the sweet odour emanating from the corpse in the coffin.

The compassionless eyes of the man shifted their attention from the woman to the remains in the casket. He had been dead several days and decomposition was already beginning to win over the work of the mortician. He looked ready to crumble into dust at any moment. But the more recently dead priest was a more horrifying sight – to anyone capable of experiencing horror. For he had died by an act of body-shattering violence, whereas the older man seemed to have passed away peacefully.

A groan caused the man to swing his head around and look at the woman again. She rolled on to her side and started to raise her naked torso, supporting herself with shaking arms and hands. Her eyes as she met the man's steady gaze seemed dead for a stretched second. Until his voice triggered her into an expression of pain and confusion: as if she could not believe the man and the horse were real until he spoke.

'Ain't true what they say, ma'am,' he murmured, and touched

21

the brim of his hat in a polite but incongruous gesture of greeting.

'What . . . ?' she managed to gasp before her vomit-caked lips trembled to cut off the rest of the intended query.

'No fate's worse than death.' He spat on to the shovel and the sun-heated metal exploded a hiss from the evaporating saliva.

The start of anger showed in her eyes now. They were green eyes. 'You saw what . . . what happened to . . . to me?' she croaked.

She swung up on to her naked rump and wiped away some of the vomit on her jaw with the back of a hand. Then she folded up her legs to press her thighs against her breasts. She clasped both arms around her knees, grasping the only degree of modesty available to her.

The man jerked a thumb up towards the cave-featured hillside. 'Had a grandstand view, ma'am.'

'And did nothing?' The anger was laced with contempt as she spat out the words, as if they tasted worse than the bile of nausea.

'Like what, ma'am?' He eased his horse into a slow wheel. 'I never interfere in other folk's business. Unless maybe I'm asked.'

He moved his horse away, to head across the rear of the hearse in the tracks left by the four departed cowhands.

'Wait!' the woman called. 'Please, Mr . . . ?'

'Name's Edge, Miss Diamond,' the man replied, halting his horse and looking back over his shoulder.

She had got to her feet and was still doing what she could to cover herself – an arm forming a bar across her punished breasts and a hand clamped over the base of her belly.

'I'll pay ten dollars if you'll help me back to Dream Creek, Mr Edge.' Fresh sweat was oozing from the pores of her face and cutting clean trails across the pasted dirt.

He hooked a leg around his saddlehorn and dug out the makings. 'I'm heading that way myself, ma'am. No charge.'

She gave a curt nod of thanks, then expressed resentment at the way Edge's narrowed eyes glinted at her from out of the

22

shade of his hat brim. 'I'd be grateful if you'd turn your back while I cover myself, Mr Edge.'

He lit the cigarette and did as she requested, then listened as she moved around to gather up her tattered clothing. He could see her shadow as she moved to the hearse and rummaged in the carpetbag. She made soft, angry sounds as she salvaged a modicum of modesty from the ruined mourning gown.

'First time for you, I guess?' he asked conversationally.

Her grunt of response was much louder. 'I was pure!' she snapped. 'Before that revolting Japanese monster touched me, it was my intention to enter heaven unviolated!'

Edge showed a wry grin which the woman could not see. 'It's the road to hell that's paved with good intentions, ma'am.'

'I would ask you to refrain from misplaced humour, Mr Edge!' she snapped. 'There, how is that?'

He swung in the saddle to look at her through a curtain of tobacco smoke. She had used hairpins to fasten the gown around her. The material fitted her more snugly than before: and even had her underwear not been left to view where it had fallen, the contours of her body would have revealed she had nothing on under the gown.

'You're decent,' Edge reported.

She shook her head emphatically. 'I'll never be that again!' She shuddered. 'Not after what that Oriental beast did to me!'

Edge sighed. 'OK, ma'am. I'll admit that in that get-up you don't look like no dew-fresh rose.' He arced his cigarette butt out into the slugglish water of the Rio Grande. Then he spat a flake of tobacco off his lower lip. 'But ain't no one can tell you been Nipped in the bud.'

Chapter Two

'YOU disgust me!' Emma Diamond shrieked at the coldly smiling man sitting nonchalantly in the saddle. 'You're as bad as they are and I don't need your help!'

She swung into a half turn, the speed of the action causing the skirt section of her gown to gape open to a point midway up her thigh. No longer concerned about exhibiting her body, she strode purposefully to the graveside and heaved the lid back on to the casket. Two of the nails were still in place and she used the shovel to hammer the lid. Then she picked up two ends of rope and tried to drag the closed casket to the brink of the hole.

It moved a mere inch and then came to a halt against a heap of dirt. She turned her sweating, straining, red-blotched face towards Edge and hissed at him between clenched teeth while she continued to haul uselessly on the ropes.

'I don't need you, I told you!' she yelled. 'Go away and leave me alone! I can do it!'

Abruptly, the patches of red enlarged to suffuse her entire

face. Her eyes grew wide, bulging like those of a spooked horse. Then they snapped close and every trace of colour drained from her face. She gave a low moan and collapsed, releasing the ropes. One leg fell limply over the side of the grave and pins popped to display the flesh from toe to hip.

Edge sighed and slid from the sadle. 'Women!' he rasped as he led the gelding down to the river bank. 'Why'd they always say the opposite of what they mean.'

He left the horse to drink and ambled over to the grave. With an easy strength, he scooped up the limp form of Emma Diamond and carried her across to the hearse. The rig supplied the only patch of shade nearby and he placed her beneath it. He did not seek anything for a makeshift pillow and he did not try to revive her from the faint before he returned to the grave.

There was no way a lone man could lower the corpse-heavy casket into the grave. So he simply dragged the pine box to the brink of the hole, hooked his heel over it and tipped it in. The corpse of Boyce Diamond hit the lid as the casket turned. An arm flopped out and was trapped between the side and partially-opened lid as the whole shebang crunched into the bottom of the grave. Dead bone broke with a dry snap.

'Apologies, feller,' Edge growled as he picked up the shovel. 'But this ain't the kind of work I usually undertake.'

He started to spade dirt back into the grave, working slowly as the exertion started to ooze sweat from his pores. The hole was not half filled in when he sensed watching eyes from the shade beneath the stalled hearse.

The man the recovered Emma Diamond appraised was somewhere in his thirties. Early or late, it was difficult to tell: for while there was certainly a quality of matured youthfulness about him, he also carried the signs of the passing years. But whether the years had been many, or simply harsh . . . there was no way of knowing. He was a tall man – six feet three inches, at least – with a build that was lean but solid. Close to two hundred pounds. The loose-limbed, easy way he worked hinted that he packed a considerable amount of strength in his frame.

Strength – and something else – was also a quality displayed by his face. A face that was lean, like his body, and burnished

25

to a dark hue by exposure to every kind of weather. But there had been a shading of the skin before the harsh sun and the bitter winds had attacked it: drawn from one line of his fore-bears. Mexican, the woman guessed correctly, basing her assumption on the jet blackness of his thick hair which reached down to his broad shoulders, and on the high cheekbones. But the icy blueness of his piercing, narrow, heavily hooded eyes told of another strain of blood coursing his veins. A father or mother with a Northern European heritage, perhaps. The hawkish nose, the firm jawline and the narrow mouth could have been inherited from either parent.

As she concentrated on the mouth, the lips slightly parted to show even, very white teeth, Emma felt herself provoked into fear. For there was a degree of cruelty apparent in the set of Edge's mouthline. She frowned, visualising anger in the blue eyes and allying it with the set of the mouth. And she realised that this was the quality in addition to strength which was displayed by the half-breed's burnished face. The man was younger than he looked. The years he had lived were fewer than they seemed at first impression. They had been hard, bitter, perhaps bloody years. Edge had undergone great suffering – and in so doing had made others suffer in return. It was as if every deep-cut line in his leather-textured skin was a notch of violence – given or received.

'I suppose rape is nothing new to you, Mr Edge!' she called at length, when he had shifted the final shovelful of dirt into the elongated heap marking the grave.

'Never did happen to me,' he answered, tossing aside the shovel and drawing the back of a hand across his sweat-sheened forehead.

'You know what I mean!' she retorted petulantly, sliding out from under the hearse and standing up. She dusted off her held-together gown as if it was still her Sunday best.

'I've seen it happen,' the half-breed replied, moving down to the river to take up the reins of his horse.

His freshly shaved face was sweat-greased and grimed from the work. His clothing – heavy-duty riding boots, narrow-legged Levis, black shirt, red kerchief and grey hat – had been worn

26

and dirty before he started. As Emma watched him hitch his tan gelding to the rear of the hearse, she guessed him to be a man who cared little for appearances. But it was obvious he took care of the revolver in the holster tied down to his right thigh and the repeater rifle jutting from his saddleboot.

'And a lot of other bad things, too, I think?' she suggested.

'It ain't a good world, ma'am,' Edge said. 'Ready?'

There was some colour back in her cheeks now. It drained away, but there was no other sign of a faint, when she glanced at the shattered body of the priest. 'I should like to take Father Donovan back to Dream Creek, Mr Edge.'

Without the bonnet to hold it in place, her blonde hair tended to swing across her face. Her green eyes implored his co-operation through the loose strands.

'How far to town?'

'About ten miles, I think.'

Edge eyed the body, on which the massive spillage of blood was already caking to a deep black: then glanced at the cloudless sky from which the sun blistered.

'That makes a long time to ride with the smell of a dead man,' he warned.

'I do not make a habit of fainting, Mr Edge,' Emma countered. 'I promise not to do it again.'

Edge spat and jerked a thumb towards the front of the hearse. 'Climb aboard,' he instructed.

She did so, after first going to the river to splash water on to her face, then retrieving her bonnet. The half-breed gathered up her tattered underwear and used it to shroud the body as much as possible. Angry flies buzzed into a departing swarm as he carried the linen-and-lace wrapped corpse to the hearse. He dumped it unceremoniously on to the casket platform in the rear and closed the doors. Then he climbed up on to the seat beside Emma and eased the team into a tight turn away from the Rio Grande.

The woman glanced over her shoulder just once before the hearse crested the shallow rise and the grave was lost to sight. She had put on the bonnet, trapping the veil to the brim. The ends of her near shoulder-length hair were tucked up under the

27

crown and this gave her a severe, almost regal look. The carpet-bag was on her knees and she delved a hand into it.

'I wish to pay you ten dollars, Mr Edge. For taking care of my father's burial after I failed.'

'No deal, ma'am,' he told her, and showed her a wry grin. 'I don't take advantage of helpless women.'

Even when he smiled, there was still a coldness about Edge: an inescapable detachment that placed him in a private world of his own while still being aware of everything around him. And, after the fleeting smile, the lines of his features returned to repose. But nonchalant relaxation as he drove the hearse was just an easy pose. Beneath this veneer, he was constantly alert and coiled to react to the unexpected. Like an animal of prey, Emma reflected, which is itself the prey of other animals.

'And you don't normally do favours for people,' she pressed.

Beyond the rise there was a broad area of sand ridges stretching to the next foothill step of the Santiagos. The tracks left by the hearse on its outward journey cut through the ridges to the west and Edge swung the team on to this course.

'Maybe it ain't a normal day,' he replied, after a lengthy pause.

Emma didn't have to think long about this. 'Rape and murder aren't new to you, Mr Edge. So it is the money that intrigues you, I suppose.'

Edge pursed his lips. 'You ain't exactly a high payer for a woman with such a rich old man.'

She responded with an angry snort, a sound that was totally out of keeping with her valiant attempt at a ladylike appearance. 'I thought so!'

The half-breed's ever-watchful eyes spotted a change in the country's pattern up ahead. The sign in the sand he was following abruptly became more confused and, at the same time, easier to see. As the slow-moving hearse rolled down into a shallow dip, he saw the reason. They had reached the point where the six grave-robbers had departed from and then rejoined the trail left by the hearse. It was at the top of a steep, shale-run embankment overlooking the sun-sparkled Rio Grande.

Mounted riders had been able to take the short-cut to the grave site. The hearse and team would not have been able to negotiate the steep, loose-surfaced slope.

'Thought so, what?' Edge asked as the wheels of the hearse began to cut clearly defined ruts in the churned-up sand.

'The money, of course!'

'Like you said, ma'am, it intrigues me.'

'It arouses your greed!' she corrected vehemently.

The outburst was greeted by silence and, when she looked at his profile, Emma saw the subtle twist to his mouthline and a cracking of his eyes that made them appear closed. But, when he turned towards her, the sun glinted on the merest slivers of ice blue. His tacit anger seemed to waft a bitter-cold airstream over her. Then, abruptly, he faced front again. His voice was evenly pitched.

'No sweat, ma'am. Your business ain't mine unless you want it to be.'

The blazing sun suddenly seemed to generate more heat than before. She smelled the overly sweet odour of Father Donovan and she patted at her sheened face with her handkerchief. She felt parched, but the only canteens were on the half-breed's horse hitched to the rear of the hearse. Vivid memories of the Jap violating her naked body crowded into her mind. She gripped the seat tightly with her gloved hands. She bit her lips with tiny teeth. The heat shimmer seemed to advance, distorting the shapes of the terrain just a few feet away. There were sharp pains between her legs, as if the brutish man was still thrusting and tearing into her.

'If you have to pass out again, I won't hold nothing against you.'

The half-breed's words sounded as if they came from a long way off: out from beyond where the shimmering heat was a wet-looking, billowing curtain. But his cynical tone was as clear as her self-knowledge that she was going to faint again. And it was terribly important not to do that. She stared directly ahead and began to talk.

'My father was Boyce Diamond,' she said slowly, her voice

29

as stiff as her body. 'The Chicago meat-packing Boyce Diamond. Before that, during the war, he was in armaments. He made a great deal of money and he died. He made a will that was explicitly simple in its terms. He wished to be buried at a particular point on the bank of the Rio Grande in Texas. And he wished all his assets to be capitalised and buried with him.'

She was speaking like a nervous child in front of a large audience, the words learned by rote and delivered without emotion.

'I intend to ensure that his wishes are carried out.' She sighed then, and the tautness drained out of her. As she sagged on the seat she looked very young, very feminine and pathetically helpless. Her tone became one of quiet determination. 'I intend to find those men, recover the money and return it to my father's coffin. And to keep within the budget of five hundred dollars he allocated for carrying out the terms of his will.'

She looked at Edge again, her firm expression warning she was ready to defend her attitude.

'Your old man didn't believe he couldn't take it with him, uh?'

'His motives are no concern of mine or anybody else's, Mr Edge.'

'How much?'

'To help me?' There was just a trace of excited anticipation in the depths of her sea green eyes. 'I have four hundred dollars of the expense money left and – '

'How much did he figure the price into heaven?' Edge cut in.

Anger returned. 'There was something over a hundred thousand dollars buried with my father!'

'Ten grand.'

'I beg your pardon?'

'If I get it back for you, ma'am.'

'Don't be ridiculous!'

'Is there a hotel in Dream Creek?'

The abrupt change of subject startled her. She blinked her long lashes. 'Why yes. I stayed there last night. The Bonnington.'

'You'll find me there if you have a change of mind, ma'am.'

30

She drew herself erect to regain her regal posture. 'I never change my mind, Mr Edge.'

'I heard it was a woman's prerogative.'

She was surprised again, by the use of a word she had not expected from a man who looked and acted like an ignorant saddletramp. 'I am not like other women,' she said after a thoughtful pause.

'Didn't see any difference back at the river,' the half-breed muttered.

'You know very well what I mean!' she snapped.

The hearse rolled around an outcrop of rock that provided a small area of shade as the sun inched towards its midday peak. Edge jerked on the reins to turn the team into the shade, then hauled on the leather to halt them.

'Why are we stopping?' Emma blurted out, with a trill of fear.

Edge swung down from the stalled hearse and narrowed his eyes against the bright sky to look up at her. 'All I got for breakfast was food for thought, ma'am,' he told her. 'And all that put in my belly was a little fire.'

'Were you burning for my body or my father's money?' she taunted as he swung away and ambled towards his horse.

The familiar chill grin turned up the corners of his mouth as he unfastened a saddlebag. 'I never mix business with pleasure.'

'You'll get neither from me!' she retorted, and flung herself around on the seat to show him her ramrod stiff back. 'You'll have more chance of getting blood from a stone!'

Edge drew from the saddlebag a waxpaper-wrapped package of sourdough bread and jerked beef. He unhooked a canteen and carried the food and water back along the side of the hearse.

'Seems to me the Jap managed to do that, Miss Diamond,' he said evenly.

She took his meaning. She could still feel the dried blood crusted on her lower belly and thighs. A grimace contorted her handsome features as she looked down at him. And she shook her head violently as he offered her a share of his meal.

'You disgust me!' she rasped as Edge dropped down on to his haunches and leaned his long back against the warm rock of

31

the outcrop. 'To take cold-blooded murder, robbery of the dead and brutal rape so lightly is . . . is . . . '

'My way, ma'am,' he completed as she became lost for words. He used a first gulp of water to rinse the dust from his mouth, then spat it out. 'In my book that wasn't such a heavy scene.'

Chapter Three

THE glass-sided hearse with its inadequately shrouded corpse rolled into Dream Creek at mid-afternoon while the sun was still high and searingly hot. There were few people on Lone Star Street or the Pecos Trail that formed a junction at the northern end of the main thoroughfare.

It was a relatively new town, its buildings a mixture of adobe and timber with the exception of the red-brick structure painted with a sign proclaiming: TEXAS SHEEPMEN'S ASSOCI-ATION. On the second leg of the trip into town – undertaken in silence after the exchange at the lunch stop – the half-breed's narrowed eyes had seen no indication of why there should be a town in the area. But then, as Dream Creek came into sight, he saw the rolling, short-grass country to the north and west of the small settlement: country that was scattered with clusters of unfenced farm buildings, with lazily moving herds of grazing sheep between.

'I wish to be let off at the office of Sheriff Schabar,' Emma Diamond said stiffly.

3

Edge had already spotted the adobe gaolhouse and law office, directly across the wide street from the Sheepmen's Association building. Next door to the three-storey, frame Bonnington Hotel and Saloon. He made no vocal response, but angled the hearse across the street towards her destination. His head swung this way and that, eyes and ears absorbing the sights and sounds of the town.

It was totally business-orientated. Lone Star Street was lined by enterprises to serve and service the needs of the people working the outlying sheep farms and any transients who happened to pass through. While the developed section of the Pecos Trail comprised only a slaughterhouse and adjacent animal pens. The people who operated the businesses lived above or out back of their premises. There were no private houses.

'Hey, is that there a body you got in the back?'

The few people who were out on Lone Star Street had paid little attention to the slow-moving hearse until a man with a reedy voice yelled the query. He was an old-timer sitting in a rocking chair on the stoop in front of the stage depot. He had been reading a newspaper, which fell to his knees and then to the boarding as he stood up.

'Hey, that's what it is, sure enough. I can smell it.'

The stage depot was alongside the red-brick building. The man – short and skinny and bespectacled – half fell off the stoop in his haste, and broke into a stiff-limbed trot across the street. Those who had heard him, turned and hurried towards the halting hearse. Some emerged from doorways or merely craned their necks to see out of windows.

'Hey, that's Donovan's rig. The one that went outta here early mornin' and . . . ' He halted level with the seat and pushed his glasses on to his forehead to peer up at the impassive Edge. 'Hey, you ain't Donovan.'

The half-breed had completed his survey of the town. The tracks of the graverobbers had marked the sandy ground all the way back to Dream Creek. But the sign had run out on the hard-packed street and there were no horses hitched out under the sun.

'Hey, where's Donovan?'

Edge jerked a thumb over his shoulder. 'Follow your nose, feller.' He turned towards Emma and touched the brim of his hat. 'You know where I'll be, ma'am.'

'Hey, that's Donovan?' The old-timer flipped his glasses across his nose again and leaned close to the side of the hearse.

As Edge swung down off the seat, the advance of the curious was halted. The smell of death reached their nostrils and they didn't have to get as close as the old-timer to recognise the shape of the hearse's freight. Men removed their hats and women crossed themselves.

'Miss Diamond, what happened?'

Edge had reached the rear of the hearse and was unhitching the gelding's reins. The plea for information was yelled by a slightly built young man in a city suit who had emerged from the Bonnington. He had stood stock still, staring at Emma as he listened to the reedy-voiced questions of the old-timer. Now he came at a run, concern etched upon his pale face with its decoration of a narrow moustache.

'Seems you, Vic, and you, Barney, are fixin' to horn in on my job.' Sheriff Schabar growled the protest as he halted on the threshold of his office. The direction of the lawman's steady gaze told Edge that the old-timer was Vic and the eighteen-year-old kid was Barney. The latter had already reached the side of the hearse and was reaching up to offer help to Emma. 'And you ain't goin' nowhere for awhile, stranger.'

Edge had started to lead the gelding around the hearse, intent upon taking him to the Bonnington Livery which was next door to the hotel. He halted and eyed Schabar levelly across the backs of the hearse team.

'You talking to me, feller?' he asked as Emma accepted Barney's hand and lowered herself to the ground, careful to hold the split skirt together.

'What do you think?'

Schabar was in his mid-forties. He was as near six feet tall as made no difference and had the well-developed build of a man who had done other things beside keep the peace in a quiet town. But he had done that for long enough to gain a padding of fat. It was thick at his belly and it weighed down the cheeks of his florid, small-eyed and wide-mouthed face. He was neatly dressed in a freshly laundered check shirt and wool pants. The thin, slicked down black hair on his head was unprotected. There was a holstered Remington on one hip and a sheathed knife on the other. But without the weapons – or the tin star on his chest – he would still have given the appearance of a bad man to tangle with.

'I think I'll stable my horse and check into the hotel, feller,' the half-breed answered.

'No objection to any of that,' Schabar offered. Then injected some flint into his dark eyes and his lazy voice. 'After I've heard what happened to our priest and mortician.'

Edge nodded. 'He died.'

He clucked to the gelding and tugged on the reins.

'Mister!' Schabar roared.

Gasps pitched low from many throats. The half-breed continued to lead his horse at a measured pace, his back to the lawman and the majority of bystanders.

'A warning, feller,' he said evenly. 'If you pull that gun on me, use it. I got this thing about pointing guns. And I got another thing – about not telling folks twice.'

'Sheriff Schabar!' Emma rasped. 'I can tell you all you need to know.'

'Hey!' Vic exclaimed his inevitable prelude to a comment. 'Donovan near enough got his head blowed off.'

'It could be catchin',' Schabar growled, then moderated his tone. 'Come inside, Miss Diamond.' Then, gruffly. 'Vic, take the priest and his property over to his place. Barney, keep an eye on the stranger and let me know if he tries to leave town. Somebody go and get Doc Adamson. He's out deliverin' the new Ellis kid.'

'Hey, Donovan's way beyond doctorin'!' the old-timer answered as he clambered up on to the hearse seat. 'Head near enough blowed off.'

'We need a certificate that he's dead, for Christsake!' the lawman snorted as he ushered Emma into his office.

Vic's mouth was hard to see through his straggly moustache and beard, which was a rich brown colour in contrast with his silver grey hair. But he was able to spit through the growth. 'Donovan ain't gonna be no deader just 'cause a sawbones signs a hunk of paper,' he mumbled as he urged the hearse team into movement.

Some of the bystanders returned to what they had been doing, exchanging low, excited conversation. A few inched towards the law office, resentful of the closed door. All cast curious, apprehensive glances towards Edge as he stopped the gelding outside the livery. Except for the smartly attired Barney, who ambled along to the batswing entrance of the hotel and surveyed his charge with officious suspicion.

'I'll take care of him for you, mister. Real good. Two dollars a day and whatever he eats.'

The leather-aproned, shiny-faced liveryman stepped out of his premises and showed his new customer a broad grin. He had tobacco-browned teeth and smelled of horse manure.

The half-breed nodded and slid his Winchester from the boot. 'He ain't a big eater so the check better not be more than three bucks a day.'

The grin faltered when it did not draw a like response. 'Sounds about right, mister. I'll bring your gear into the hotel.'

'Busy?'

'What?'

'Busy day, feller?'

The liveryman shook his head. 'No, sir. You're the first.'

'Obliged.'

Edge swung away from the man and canted the Winchester to his shoulder as he stepped up on to the hotel stoop. He towered a full head above the youthful Barney, who remained firmly on the threshold of the Bonnington.

'You plan to stay in town?' the kid asked. Like his pale grey eyes, his voice betrayed no hint of nervousness. 'When I'm given a job, I take it real seriously.'

'Way it should be,' Edge replied evenly.

'Knock it off, Barney!' a man called from inside the building. 'You ain't impressin' nobody!'

Edge looked over Barney's head of bushy blond hair. The first floor front of the Bonnington was given over to the saloon

37

area. There was a horseshoe-shaped bar with two elderly tenders behind it. Tables and chairs were liberally scattered over the rest of the space. The stairway canted up an end wall to a gallery. There was no dais for entertainment. Neither were there any gaming tables. The place was dusty, but not run down.

The man who called the warning to Barney was one of the quartet who had acted as pallbearers at the burial out on the Rio Grande bank. The four were the only customers, drinking beer and playing dominoes at a table under the gallery. Cowhands once, maybe: but their presence in Dream Creek meant they were equally willing to work with sheep. A lot of punchers were not.

'You're impressing me, kid,' the half-breed corrected after he had made his hooded-eyed survey of the saloon.

The light of a hard smile entered Barney's eyes and he swung to the side to leave the way clear for Edge. 'That's good, mister. 'Cause I can take care of myself when the stuff hits the fan. Get me?'

Edge took a step forward, then swung fast from the waist. The man who had given the warning groaned. Barney caught his breath and streaked a hand under his jacket. The half-breed's free hand was faster. It rose from his side and then shot forward, the long, brown fingers forming into a claw. The fingers closed over Barney's lapels and bunched them together, trapping the kid's hand between his wrist and the top button of the coat. There was frustration rather than fear in the pale grey eyes as the kid struggled to get his gun out. As his other hand sprang up to claw at Edge's wrist, the half-breed reached around Barney and calmly leaned his Winchester against the held-open door.

'I got you.'

'He talks big is all!' another of the domino-playing hands pleaded.

'That's how you impress me, kid,' Edge rasped at the struggling Barney.

'I got a job to do!' the youngster croaked. 'The sheriff ain't gonna like this.'

38

'Sheriff had sense enough not to talk himself into it, kid. Let go of the gun.'

'So you can beat me up?' Barney taunted. He met the steady gaze from the ice-blue eyes of the half-breed. But still he was not afraid. Then he caught his breath again. When Edge's right hand was drawn back, Barney expected to feel a bunched fist smash into his face. Instead, the hand went from sight for an instant, reaching under the thick black hair at the nape of the half-breed's neck. When the hand showed, it was wrapped around the wooden handle of an open razor drawn from a neck pouch. Barney's pent-up breath was expelled in a subdued scream of terror. When the blade was rested on his flesh, at one end of his narrow moustache, the sound was curtailed. His Adam's apple bobbed.

'Jesus, mister, he don't deserve that.' This from one of the bartenders.

'I dropped it, I dropped it!' Barney croaked.

Edge responded with a curt nod and loosened his grip on the jacket lapels. A small .32 Tranter six-shot revolver slipped from under the coat and bounced off Barney's shoe to the floor.

'There, mister!'

'Obliged,' Edge said. Then, deliberately, he angled the razor blade into the flesh and drew it sideways.

The finely-honed steel peeled off a thin sliver of skin from one side of Barney's mouth to the other, removing the embryo moustache. A flick of the razor arced the displaced skin out from the saloon on to the dusty street. A bright smear of blood showed beneath Barney's nose, and oozed down over his trembling lips.

'That's the closest shave you're ever likely to get kid,' Edge muttered as he released the youngster, picked up his rifle and stepped away. 'Without dying.'

He swung and walked towards the bar. Barney staggered to the nearest table and dropped heavily on to a chair. He dabbed at his face with a handkerchief and stared in disbelief at the crimson staining on the white linen.

'I dropped the damn gun!' he yelled at the half-breed's back. 'You didn't have to do this to me!'

'Beer,' Edge told one of the bartenders. He ran each side of the bloodied blade down the angle of the bar and replaced the razor in the sheath that was held at the nape of his neck by a beaded thong.

'That was pretty mean, mister,' the shorter of the bartenders growled as he set down a foam-topped glass of beer.

'Sure was!' one of the hands agreed sourly. 'Barney just talks up he's a big man.'

'Obliged,' the half-breed told the bartender, and swallowed a great gulp of the cold beer. He showed a quiet grin of enjoyment as the dust of the long trip was washed from his throat.

'Ain't no one takes him serious,' the other bartender added.

'Shuddup, you bastards!' Barney shrieked, reaching down to scoop up his Tranter. He glared around at the pitying faces of his sympathisers and thrust the gun back into his shoulder rig. 'I still ain't scared of him. I'm stayin' right here to see he don't leave town. Just like the sheriff told me. I take my work serious!'

Edge finished the rest of the beer at a single swallow. 'Like a room.'

The man who had served him the beer reached under the bar and produced a key. There was heavy contempt in his age-glazed eyes. 'Price of the beer will go on the bill, mister.'

'And I'm here to make sure he don't leave without paying you, Seth!' Barney warned as the half-breed headed between the scattering of tables towards the foot of the stairway.

'Knock it off, Barney!' the beefiest hand advised harshly. 'You already tangled with him over nothin'. And what did it get you, you crazy kid!'

'It proved I got guts, that's what!' Barney retorted savagely. 'Somethin' nobody in this town'd ever believe before.'

'Yeah, and he give you the scar to prove it, lunkhead!' Seth growled.

'Right, feller,' Edge called down from the gallery as Barney stared hatefully up towards him. 'Everyone can see you're a cut above the rest.'

Chapter Four

THE half-breed had stayed in hotels that were both better and worse than the Bonnington. But few that were quieter. Which made the place representative of the town. Dream Creek – named for the shallow stream that meandered down from the grazing land, crossed the Pecos Trail and ran parallel with Lone Star Street before its final course to the Rio Grande – returned to a state of placid lethargy after the tall, taciturn, lean-faced stranger went to his room.

Strong feelings were expressed between people meeting on the street or gathering in the places of business. Sadness for the violent death of Father Donovan. Sympathy for Emma Diamond who had obviously suffered a severe shock. Anger at Edge for what he had done to the tough-talking but harmless Barney Castle. And an all-engulfing resentment at the trouble which strangers had caused to spill over into Dream Creek. But, strong as these feelings ran, they were kept low-keyed.

All who lived in town, and those who came in from the scattered farms to learn the news, had experienced his or her share of trouble in the past. They were sheep people in the cattle land of Texas who, in this border strip, had found a peaceful haven to go about their business without constant harassment from range-hungry beef-raisers. Now the threat of violence was looming over them once more and they were anxious not to instigate it into reality by their own actions.

So, as the gloom of evening spread in from the east, seeming to speed the setting sun over the rim of the western horizon, the people in Dream Creek talked and wondered and hoped their fears would not be realised.

As the day drew to a close and night took a first, tentative grip on the town and surrounding country, Edge slept on the narrow bed in the tiny back room on the hotel's second floor. He slept with his boots off and his hat tipped forward over his face: and with the Winchester on the floor, his right arm draped over the side of the bed, relaxed hand folded around the frame.

It was a sleep that was both restful and shallow: restoring expended energy to a weary body while a part of his mind remained actively alert. Twice he almost resurfaced to total waking: both times occasioned by the sound of footfalls on the gallery outside his room door. First, a man approached and halted. Edge's hand tightened its grip on the Winchester. Something heavy was dropped to the floor.

'Your gear, sir!' the liveryman called.

The hammer in the half-breed's mind which would have tripped him into full alertness, total recall and instant action, was returned to rest.

Later, he heard the lighter tread of a woman nearing his door. But she went on by, and entered the next room. He was aware of a voice. Speaking softly, but recognisable as Emma Diamond. The words she spoke did not penetrate the thin party wall. Their tone did, and suggested the woman was praying. But choking sobs stemmed the flow. It took her a long time to control her emotions.

After that the half-breed resumed his dreamless sleep undisturbed until he awoke naturally.

Moonlight shafted in through the curtainless window. It was open and the smell of cooking food rose from below and wafted into the room. The aroma made him hungry for a meal that was not dried or canned or stale. But first he hauled in his gear from outside and found some soap. With it, he was able to get a degree of lather from the bowl of dusty water on the lopsided bureau under the window. He stripped to the waist and washed. A hand drawn across his jaw erupted a rasping sound from the tough bristles, but he gave eating a higher priority than shaving. So he dressed, canted the Winchester to his right shoulder and left the room to go down into the saloon.

A strong smell of stale liquor and a layer of blue tobacco smoke clinging to the raftered ceiling revealed that business had been good. But not any more. Just one table was occupied, close to the top curve of the horseshoe-shaped bar. Barney Castle sat on one side, a strip of blood-stained sticking plaster along his top lip. He was eating a dish of stew. Opposite him, Emma Diamond seemed to be in a melancholy trance as she stared into space and constantly stirred a full but no longer steaming mug of coffee. She was wearing a grey dress patterned on similar lines to the mourning gown.

The kid lost his appetite when he saw Edge descending the stairway. He said something to Emma, but did not get through to her until he touched her hand. She snatched it away from him as if he had hurt her. Then turned her head to look towards Edge. The disgust expressed by her green eyes was strongly overshadowed by the hatred of Barney's gaze.

'Be obliged for a bowl of the stew, feller,' the half-breed called to Seth, who was the only bartender on duty now.

'Sure,' Seth growled, as if he wished he could offer a different kind of response. 'But I'd be obliged if you didn't start no more trouble.'

'Starting it isn't my way, feller. Finish it when I have to.'

The bartender shuffled out through a beaded archway behind the bar as Edge sat at a table and leaned his Winchester against his chair.

'I think it is terrible,' Emma said. 'What you did to Barney.'

'Don't fret, Miss Diamond,' the kid urged, made to reach out and touch her hand again, but drew back. His tone toughened. 'I can take care of what concerns me.'

She appeared not to hear him. She returned to stirring her cold coffee. 'It further demonstrates what kind of a brute and a coward you are.'

'Coward?' Barney said eagerly, his gaze darting between the woman and the half-breed. 'What does that mean, Miss Diamond? What really happened this mornin'?'

'Hey, that's right, young 'un!' the bearded Vic yelled as he pushed in through the batswings, closed now against a dust-raising night wind that had sprung out of the mountains to the north. 'You ask the lady that. 'Cause Sheriff Schabar sure ain't gonna satisfy no curiosity. Got somethin' to do with them six hard eggs that was through here, I'm bettin'.'

He was ignored as he crossed to the bar, polishing the lenses of his glasses and then hurriedly replacing them on his nose.

'What d'you mean, Miss Diamond?' Barney demanded.

Vic banged a fist on the bartop. 'Hey, let me have a beer! Thirsty work, diggin' Donovan's grave.'

For a while, Emma seemed lost in her trancelike state again. Then, while continuing to stir the coffee, she replied to the query. Her voice was flat and totally lacking in emotion. But this somehow had the effect of coating each word with ugly venom.

'He just stood and watched. He had a grandstand view, he said.'

'Hey, of what?' Vic urged.

'Shuddup, you old fool!' Barney ordered. His hard eyes flicked to Emma's bowed head, then swung to stare fixedly at Edge.

'The men came. They dug up my father's body. And one of them . . . one of them attacked me. Father Donovan tried to intervene. To stop the . . . the attack. He was shot down.'

'Here's your stew, mister,' Seth growled as he pushed through the beads and banged the bowl down on to the bartop.

'Shuddup!' Barney yelled, the veins standing out like throbbing worms at his temples and neck. Violet worms against the crimson of his skin.

'What the – ' Seth started.

'Woman reckons the stranger's yeller,' Vic whispered, holding on his glasses with fingertips against each sidepiece.

For stretched seconds, the scrape of the spoon against the mug and the slopping of the coffee were the only sounds within the saloon. Outside, footfalls pounded against the hard-packed surface of the street.

'Then the men rode off. And Edge came down from the grandstand.'

Barney Castle sprang to his feet. His chair crashed over on to its side.

'Hold it!' Schabar bellowed as his footfalls thudded on to the stoop and the batswings were flung aside by his meaty hands.

'Dear God, no!' Emma screamed.

'Hey – ' Vic started.

'Crazy fool!' Seth yelled.

The kid reached under his coat and cocked the Tranter as the barrel cleared the lapel.

All within a second, the actions and words a confused tableau of sights and sounds. And the half-breed waited for that second to be expended, his nonchalant exterior a pose behind which he was tensed for retaliation. His hands were flat on the table, except for his thumbs which were curled beneath the curved rim. His feet were flat on the floor. And that was how every pair of eyes saw him as they swung in his direction: the instant the Tranter was levelled at him and the kid's knuckle whitened around the trigger.

Then he powered his hands upwards, forced his feet hard against the floor, and threw himself sideways off the chair.

'Hit the deck, lady!'

Seth's words were loud enough to be heard against the crack of the .32 bullet exploded from the Tranter's muzzle. The slug tore into the top of the table as Edge tipped it forward. He hit the floor before his falling chair and his Colt was clear of the holster while he was still going down. He fired from the right hip as his left shoulder was jarred by the impact of the fall. Barney Castle took the bullet as he swung his gun and cocked it. The range was no more than twenty feet and the .44 slug did not run out of velocity until it buried itself in the far wall of the saloon. Tiny droplets of blood were flung down the smoke-

45

soiled woodwork as it impacted. Larger splashes of bright crimson were exploded from the entry and exit wounds in the front and rear of Barney's head. The trajectory was always upwards: from close to the floor, across the intervening gap, into the kid's jaw, through his tongue, across the back of his throat, into his lower brain and finally out through the back of his skull. His dying sound was a ghastly gargle. Blood was the mouthwash, and it spurted from his gaping lips in a saliva-speckled torrent as he flipped over backwards and smashed down to the floor.

Emma screamed, curtailed it, crossed herself, clasped her hands and mouthed a silent prayer.

Vic took off his glasses and cleared the lenses of the steam of excitement. 'Hey, feller, that's the fastest draw and killin' shot I ever did see!'

Edge climbed to his feet, spun the Colt's cylinder, ejected the spent cartridge and took a fresh one from his gunbelt to reload. Then he holstered the gun, dusted off the sawdust from his pants and shirt, retrieved his fallen Winchester and took a seat at another table.

'Hey, and so damn cool with it!' the old-timer hissed as Schabar went to squat at the side of Barney.

'Like my stew's getting to be,' Edge said evenly. 'Mind passing it over here, feller?'

'Take it to him, Vic!' the lawman ordered as he rose from his examination of the body. 'Then go dig another grave.'

The old-timer hurried to bring the bowl of food and a spoon to Edge. 'Hey, my opinion is that you ain't yeller, mister. I – '

'Dig the damn grave!' Schabar roared.

Vic grimaced to an extent where his glasses almost fell off as he scampered towards the batswings. There, he halted for a final comment. 'Hey!' he exclaimed defiantly. 'It's true he ain't yeller. Let Barney draw and get the drop on him before he – '

'Dig the damn grave!' Schabar repeated, his tone lower but the hardness of his expression warning the short-sighted old-timer that he would take no more argument.

Vic muttered a string of curses, but pushed out between the batswings and elbowed his way through the knot of people who had come on the run in response to the shots. These people nudged and jostled each other for a clear view into the saloon, but none stepped across the threshold. The night wind found entrance over their heads and between their legs. It swung the ceiling-hung kerosene lamps and eddied patches of the sawdust sprinkled on the floor.

'You're one lucky guy, Edge!' the lawman announced, angling to the bar. It required only a nod to the bartender for Seth to reach for a bottle of whiskey. The other elderly tender, drawn from beyond the beaded archway by the shooting, set up the glass. The amber liquid made a lot of noise passing from the bottle into the glass.

'Luck is for fellers who don't have anything else going for them, Sheriff,' the half-breed answered. His narrowed eyes met the lawman's small ones. The gazes remained locked for a second, both colder than the wind from the north. Then Schabar gulped at his whiskey and Edge continued spooning up his stew.

'I don't mean about cuttin' down Barney Castle, Edge. He asked for it – a hot-tempered kid tanglin' with a cool number like you. You're just lucky I happened to be around to see it happen.'

'I wasn't selling tickets, feller.'

Schabar poured the rest of the liquor into his wide mouth, then slammed the glass back down on to the bar top. He covered it with a meaty hand when Seth stepped forward to offer a refill.

'You got a mouth that's as smart as the rest of you, Edge!' he snapped. 'But that don't bother me. It does bother me that Barney's dead, but you got the best eye-witness there is that it was a clear case of self-defence. So ain't nothin' I can do but fix up a decent funeral for him. That, and tell you to get out of Dream Creek first thing in the mornin'. On account that you got no place here, Edge.'

The half-breed finished the stew. 'Like a beer to wash down the food,' he told the bartenders.

'This is a nice, quiet town where folks go about their business and don't cause no trouble for other folks,' Schabar continued. 'And a man like you got no place in that.'

Seth drew the beer and banged the foaming glass on the bar-top, the gesture and his expression making it plain he had no intention of bringing it to the table. Edge rose, canted the Winchester to his shoulder and went to the bar. He smiled coldly at Seth, who backed off two paces.

'You're lucky, Sheriff,' he said after swallowing some beer.

'My feelin' about luck is the same as yours, mister,' the law-man barked, then glowered at the group in the doorway. 'Two of you men take Barney over to Donovan's place!' he snapped. 'Rest of you folks go home. Ain't nothin' else to see.'

Emma Diamond looked up suddenly, her prayer finished. There was deep shock on her pale face as she watched two men advance into the saloon and gingerly pick up the inert form of the kid.

'I'm sorry,' she whispered, and looked guiltily around her. When her green eyes located Edge, they found a brief resting place. And her spoken apology became tacit and even more heart-felt.

'What d'you mean?' Schabar asked. His tiny eyes showed curiosity as he looked at Edge sipping the beer.

'You haven't got a problem, feller. Lamb chops are the only thing I like about sheep. And the hotel service is lousy. I got no reason at all to stay in town.'

Seth grimaced and Schabar hitched up his pants around his bulging waistline as he vented a satisfied grunt.

'That's just fine,' the lawman answered. 'And, just for the record, I didn't need to talk to you about what happened to Donovan out to the east. Miss Diamond supplied me with a full report.'

'And received nothing in return!' the woman said grimly, using her hands hooked over the edge of the table to push herself erect.

Schabar's mouth twitched as a sign that he was controlling a threat of rising anger.

'And you also made sure that nobody else here would help me!' Emma added in the same tone.

She swung around, the skirts of her gown swishing. Her footfalls crossing the floor and mounting the stairway were louder than the shuffling tread of the men carrying the corpse out of the saloon.

Schabar stabbed a shaking hand towards the two men and their burden. 'Him and Donovan, lady!' he rasped. 'They'd both be alive if you hadn't brought killin' trouble to Dream Creek! And we don't want no more of the same kind! He pushed his bulky form away from the bar to trail the corpse. 'Tomorrow mornin', Edge!' he snapped.

'Wrong, Sheriff!' the half-breed called.

Schabar came to an abrupt halt and whirled, right hand dropping to drape over the butt of his holstered Remington. The redness of his face shaded towards purple.

'No more, please,' Emma gasped, coming to a halt halfway up to the gallery.

'What the hell, mister?' the lawman demanded, eyes boring into the back of Edge as the half-breed finished his beer.

'How much I owe you, feller?' Edge asked Seth. 'The beers, the stew and the room?'

'I asked you a question!' Schabar roared.

'Five dollars even if you're outta the room before 10 am,' Seth said dully.

Edge drew a slender bankroll from his hip pocket and counted off four ones. He dropped the bills on the bartop. 'Five minutes to get my gear out and you can rent the room again, feller,' he said.

'Oh!' Emma exclaimed loudly, then turned and lifted her skirts to run up the rest of the stairs.

The tension drained out of the two bartenders and the sheriff.

'That's even better than I'd hoped for,' Schabar rasped.

'Like to spread a little happiness,' Edge answered as he turned from the bar and smiled coldly at the lawman, who was still handling his gun butt – without serious intent now. Then his hand dropped away fast as he met the half-breed's narrowed eyes and saw they were completely devoid of the humour which turned up the corners of the thin mouthline.

'You sure told him his fortune, Burt!' Seth growled as Edge started up the stairway in the wake of Emma Diamond.

Schabar spat into the sawdust. 'Save your praise for them that deserves it! He ain't runnin' on account of me. He don't scare. And he don't do nothin' unless he's got a good reason.'

The lawman turned and pushed out through the batswings. There was no knot of bystanders to act as a windbreak now and an icy blast burst into the saloon. The sawdust was lifted and tumbled into minor drifts around table and chairlegs. Except for the patches pasted to the floor by the drying blood of Barney Castle.

'Ain't no good reason for a man to go out ridin' open country on a night like this one!' Seth's bartending partner growled.

Seth scooped up the used glasses and plunged them into a bowl of scummy water beneath the bartop. 'You care, Jim?' he asked.

Jim clawed the four bills off the bar and dropped them into the cash-drawer. 'Guess I don't at that, Seth. He paid what he owed and that's an end to it.'

Seth nodded and glanced up the stairway as Edge moved out of sight beyond the gallery rail. 'Just be grateful money was all he owed us.'

Upstairs, there were no lamps in the hallway leading off the gallery. But an overspill from the swaying lamps lighting the saloon took total blackness out of the dark. Emma's grey dress and paler colour of her face showed her position clearly in the doorway of her room.

'Mr Edge, I'd like to do business with you,' she said nervously. 'Will you act like a gentleman if I invite you into my room?'

He halted outside his own door. 'How much?'

She swallowed hard. 'Half what you wanted.'

His teeth gleamed in the poor light. 'Ain't a complete woman worth five grand, ma'am,' he said lightly.

'You know what I'm talking about!' Emma snapped, then lowered her voice. 'I want you to – '

'You've had enough of that kind of excitement for one day, ma'am,' he told her as he swung open his door.

50

'Well, I've never been so insulted in my life!' she exclaimed.

He stepped across the threshold of his room. 'Must be because you don't get out much,' he answered, and kicked the door closed.

Chapter Five

'I HEARD you was leavin', so I got him ready for you,' the shiny-faced liveryman said as Edge entered the stables a few minutes later. He showed his teeth – as brown as his apron – in a broad grin that did not quite conceal his dislike for the half-breed.

A pot-bellied stove was glowing bright red, keeping the cold of the night out of the fetid stables.

'Whoever kept a secret in a small town?' Edge asked as he checked the saddle cinch and tested the set of the bridle. He discovered the liveryman knew his job and gave him three dollars.

'Weren't never a secret were it?' the man asked as Edge slid the Winchester into the boot.

'But this town can keep them if it wants to,' Emma Diamond said savagely as she slid in through the door, letting a wedge of cold air enter with her. She slammed the door and leaned her back against it. Strands of wind-blown hair fell from under her bonnet and she rubbed her gloved hands together. She was wearing a thick topcoat with the collar turned up. 'I'll meet your terms, Mr Edge. Ten thousand. But you'll have to return the money to me first. I do not have your fee.'

The liveryman was surprised by her sudden appearance, and confused by what she said. Edge accepted the deal with a curt nod. Then tightened his mouthline as the wind made a howling sound along a Dream Creek alley.

'Been easier earned money if the job had come before the wind, ma'am.'

'I think Mr Florin can point us in the right direction, Mr Edge,' Emma said. There was hardness in her green eyes as she fixed the liveryman with a stare.

'You Florin?' Edge asked.

The liveryman swallowed hard and nodded. 'Sure, but I don't know nothin' more than any other folks in town.'

'But you're handier than they are,' the half-breed pointed out, turning to face Florin.

When he sweated, the liveryman smelled even more strongly of horse-manure. His eyes darted from Edge to Emma and back again. He stepped away, and came up against the front of a stall.

'You asked around already?' Edge said.

'Earlier,' Emma replied, and she no longer sounded so confident. Florin, who was as tall as the half-breed and a great deal heavier with excess fat, was trembling a little. 'I spoke to several people, but the elderly gentleman with the beard and the glasses was the only one who'd talk to me. He said to ask Mr Florin about the man with the withered arm. But Mr Florin said he knew nothing.'

'I don't know nothin' – honest!' the liveryman insisted, turning his pleading stare towards Emma. 'Why should I know anythin' more than any other folks?'

'And what's that?' Edge asked.

'What?'

'That other folks know?'

'About the men?'

'For a start.' Edge leaned against a roof support post and took out the makings.

53

'And an end!' Florin countered, failing to draw more than a sympathetic frown from Emma. 'Sheriff Schabar told us all not to say nothin', mister. Said all it'd do would bring more killin' trouble to Dream Creek.'

Edge fired the cigarette and carefully pinched out the flame before dropping the used match to the straw-covered floor. 'Which way did they go, feller?'

'When they come back?'

'Know the way they went when they went?' He blew smoke into the sweat-sheened face of Florin.

Florin licked his lips and grimaced at the salt taste. 'South, mister. South. Down along the creek and across the river, I guess. Down into greaseball land.'

'Mexico,' Edge said, softly but with unconcealed meanness in the single word.

'What I meant, mister.'

Edge made to bring the cigarette back up to his lips. Instead, he thrust his hand suddenly forward. The stall front kept Florin from drawing back any further. He tried to bring up both his hands to protect himself, but he was no match for the half-breed. The wind howled down the alley. Emma vented a strangled scream through the hands clamped to her mouth. Florin gave a gasp of pain as the glowing end of the cigarette seared for an instant in the hollow of his throat before the fire was extinguished on his sweat-run flesh.

'Say what you mean!' Edge rasped as he snatched his hand away and Florin clawed at his throat.

Florin was speechless with pain and anger for a moment. Then, showing that he could command speed of his own when it was demanded, he shot his hands high over his head to fist them around the shaft of a pitchfork sticking out of the hayloft above the stalls.

'You bastard!' he shrieked, yanking downwards and dropping hard to his haunches.

'Oh, no!' Emma yelled.

With the edge of the hayloft as a fulcrum, the pitchfork whipped downwards, its curved tines smashing towards the half-breed's head. The gelding shied away and Edge flung himself to the side. The powerful momentum of the down-swinging pitchfork did not allow Florin to alter the direction of its flight. A groan of frustration ripped from his compressed lips as the tines crashed against the floor. Edge smacked into the hindquarters of the frightened horse and bounced off. His left foot came down hard on the tines of the pitchfork. He swung his right leg hard to the side and slammed it down an instant later. Florin screamed as his fisted hands were trapped between the shaft and the floor.

He ripped them free, leaving the blood-stained skin of stripped knuckles on the floor. Then he tried to rise and run. Edge took his right foot off the pitchfork and slid his left along the curves of the tines. The shaft sprang off the floor and slammed into Florin's crotch as the man attempted the first stride of his panicked escape. His scream was high and short, and became a groan as he went full length to the floor and then jack-knifed, clutching at his new injury.

'No!' Emma pleaded, flinging herself away from the door to run towards Edge.

'Please?' Florin added as he caught a glimpse of the half-breed through tear-misted eyes.

But Edge ignored both pleas as he continued the movement he had started. He had already picked up the pitchfork in both hands and pushed it high above his head. Now he took two steps forward and drove it downwards. Emma pulled up short with a dry sob. Florin became petrified by terror. His mouth gaped wide, but no sound emerged. The pitchfork made a soft, hissing noise as it approached his head, still firmly gripped by the half-breed.

There was no glint from the rusted points of the tines. A dull thud as they drove home, burying themselves deeply into the dirt floor of the stable.

Emma listened for the man's dying scream and failed to hear it. She snapped open her eyes and let out her breath in a body-shuddering gasp. Florin coughed. It expanded his throat, and the flesh at the nape of his neck and beneath his jaw touched the cold metal of the two tines trapping him to the floor.

'Say what you mean, feller,' Edge repeated softly, and there was no trace of anger in his voice or attitude as he released his grip on the pitchfork and dropped to his haunches beside the trapped head of Florin.

'What'd I say?' the liveryman croaked. He was only able to raise his head an inch off the floor.

'That's Mexican land across the river, feller,' Edge supplied. 'My Pa was a Mexican. Also happens he married my Ma before he did what was necessary for her to have me.'

'Gee, mister,' Florin croaked. 'How was I supposed to know you were so touchy?'

'You know now?'

Florin gave a necessarily restricted nod.

Edge raked a fingernail along one of the tines. 'Made my pitch about what he didn't know of my family, ma'am. What is he supposed to know about yours?'

The woman was breathing deeply as she struggled to recover from the shock of the sudden eruption of violence. 'There was a man here,' she replied in a rasping voice. 'With a withered left arm. That's all the elderly gentleman told me. Will you ask Mr Florin about him, please?'

'You heard her,' Edge said.

Florin gulped. 'Vic's crazy, mister. Everyone in Dream Creek knows that. You give him any money, Miss Diamond?'

'I'll allow I gave him five dollars,' the woman admitted. 'But I – '

'Then that explains it,' Florin cut in, massaging his crotch and wincing. 'Vic'll do most anythin' for a couple of bucks.'

'You mention a withered arm to the old-timer?' Edge asked the woman.

'No. No, I didn't, but I know – '

Edge drew the razor from its neck pouch and Emma caught her breath again. Florin watched in horrified fascination as the half-breed ran a finger along the gleaming blade.

'Five is more than a couple, feller. But even the extra three wouldn't give the old-timer an imagination. He didn't pull a man with a withered arm out of nowhere.'

'Ask him about it, for Christsake!' Florin defended.

'Feller's busy,' Edge countered, and rested the point of the

56

blade gently in Florin's uppermost ear. 'Be even busier if I have to talk to him.'

'I won't countenance further brutality, Mr Edge!' Emma snapped. 'I'd rather do things my way!'

'You tried your way, ma'am,' Edge reminded.

There was a pause, then the woman came forward and squatted down alongside Edge. 'Please tell him, Mr Florin,' she begged. 'It is the most important thing in life to me.'

'Hell!' Florin rasped sourly. 'I ain't gonna die just 'cause Burt Schabar's a worrier. The guy with the bum arm rode into Dream Creek three days ago. He was hungry and he was broke and I gave him a job cleanin' up for me. And let him sleep up in the loft.'

'Name?' Edge asked, maintaining the threat with the razor.

'Tom was all he said.'

The half-breed glanced at Emma, but the name drew no reaction from her. She was still looking disgusted at taking part in the interrogation. Edge nodded for the suffering liveryman to continue.

'Then, this mornin', the six other strangers come in.'

'After Father Donovan and I and the men I hired left with my father's body?' Emma asked.

'Right, ma'am. And before most folks was up and about.' He was not sweating so much now: seemed relieved that he could ease his mind with talking. 'But me, I've always been an early riser. Came outta the hotel and saw my stable door was open. Inside – in here – the six guys were drinkin' coffee Tom made for them. And their nags were havin' breakfast on my hay.'

'Scared?' Edge asked.

'Sure was, mister. Mean-lookin' bunch. Specially the tall guy – taller than you and me, even. And a fat Jap.'

Emma shuddered, but bit her lower lip to hold in a vocal response.

'Them?'

'Nervous, I'd guess you'd say,' Florin answered the half-breed. 'Give me fifty dollars, though. Said it was for the coffee and feed – and to forget I'd seen them. Then they left. Walked their nags out beyond town. Real quiet like.'

57

'What about Tom?' Emma asked.

'He stayed,' Edge said.

'How'd you know that?' Florin wanted to know.

'They had to have some reason to come back to Dream Creek. To pick him up?'

Florin nodded, banging his chin against the pitchfork tine. 'They did that, all right. Come in as quiet and easy as they went out. Tom had his broken down old mare saddled and ready to ride. He'd been watchin' for them better than a couple of hours. He saw them comin' and he was out on the street, mounted and waitin'. And they left together.'

'A number of people saw them, Mr Edge,' Emma supplied. 'But that's all they would say. They saw them come into Dream Creek and then leave again – going in a southerly direction.'

She straightened up and a small bone in her leg cracked after being under prolonged tension in one position.

'Burt Schabar told them to say that, ma'am,' Florin said quickly as Edge continued to squat and hold the razor against the prisoner's ear. 'But it was west they rode. Out along the Pecos Trail.'

'Obliged, feller,' Edge said as he rose and returned the razor to its neck pouch.

'Why?' Emma asked as the half-breed fisted his hands around the shaft of the pitchfork and withdrew the tines from the dirt floor.

Florin eased himself up into a sitting position. Despite the curious stare of the woman, he continued to massage his injured crotch. But his hands worked under cover of his apron.

'He had his reason, Miss Diamond. See, he recognised Conrad Andrews. That's the big guy – the tall one. Wanted posters out on him. Seems he's a real mean guy who don't care who he kills to get what he wants. But Andrews didn't do nothin' here in town. And what was done to you and Donovan, Miss Diamond . . . well, that was outside Burt Schabar's jurisdiction. Well, he said the best way to keep Andrews and his gang from doin' nothin' in town was not to help you, ma'am. On account that, if we did, Andrews would find out about it and come back to Dream Creek.'

'That's a terrible attitude for a peace officer to take!' Emma exclaimed. 'And you and the rest of the people here are no better, Mr Florin!'

The liveryman showed an expression of hurt that had nothing to do with his physical injuries. Then he eyed Edge curiously as he defended himself and his fellow-citizens.

'You got to see it from our point of view, Miss Diamond. And, you being from the east and all, I guess it ain't easy . . . '

Edge was moving about the stable, checking the beat-up desk in the corner, looking into stalls and tapping the walls with his knuckles.

' . . . But we got us a nice, quiet town. Which wasn't easy to come by for folks that deal in sheep. And we went through a lot of trouble before we got it – '

'I know all about that, Mr Florin!' Emma cut in. 'Everyone in Dream Creek has had a terrible time in the past. But you just can't say you've had enough and surrender to law-breakers and murderers. Why, if everyone did that, there would never be any places like Dream Creek and – '

'What the hell you lookin' for, Edge?' Florin demanded.

'Place you keep your money,' the half-breed answered.

Anger coloured Florin's face and he hauled himself painfully to his feet. He had to bend slightly from the waist to quell the full impact of the pain from his crotch. 'You gonna rob me, too?' he demanded.

'That, I will not condone!' Emma flung at Edge.

He ignored both of them as he returned to the battered desk. He noticed that there was bare dirt at one side of it, whereas the rest of the floor was covered with strewn straw. He laid his Winchester across the desktop, hooked his fingers under the edge and pulled. The desk slid over the floor area free of straw – to expose a shallow hole sunk into the dirt. A rusted tin cashbox lay in the bottom of the hole.

'Mr Edge!' Emma snapped in high anger.

Florin glanced towards the discarded pitchfork, but immediately dismissed it. Then he glared helplessly at his rifle held by brackets to the wall above the desk.

'You figure to ride with me, ma'am?' the half-breed asked as

59

he flipped open the lid of the unlocked box.

'I had intended to,' Emma allowed. 'But I am now having second thoughts about our arrangement.'

The box held a mixture of bills and coinage. Edge estimated there was no more than five hundred dollars in all. He took out two twenties and a ten, returned the box to the hole and slid the desk back into its accustomed position. The anger of both the watchers ebbed a little. He picked up his Winchester, went to the gelding and slid the rifle into the saddleboot.

'Doing you a favour, feller,' he told Florin. 'You keep this fifty bucks and you're guilty of aiding and abetting the commission of grave-robbery and murder.'

'Some damn favour!' the liveryman snarled. 'You're the one that gains from it!'

'You having any third thoughts about our arrangement, ma'am?' Edge asked Emma.

She attempted to hide her helplessness behind a shield of tight-lipped silence. Edge waited for only a second, then shrugged and allowed the three bills to flutter to the floor as he took hold of the gelding's reins and led the animal towards the door.

'I'll be on the Pecos Trail,' he supplied. 'Riding west. You'll need a horse.' He nodded towards a row of three occupied stalls at the rear of the stables. 'The black gelding is the best if he's for sale. Some clothes that are more hard-wearing than the dress. And supplies. Canned and dried.'

'I have my own money to pay my own way!' Emma replied stiffly.

'It's all right, Miss Diamond!' Florin said quickly. 'You use that fifty. Now I know what Andrews and his bunch done, I wouldn't feel right keepin' it for nothin'.'

'Please wait for me, Mr Edge,' Emma called as the half-breed opened the door to admit a further blast of icy air from the north. It swayed the single lamp, caused the stove to roar, and stirred up the fallen bills.

'But I'll take the fifty for the black geldin',' Florin offered, trapping the money under his foot.

'Time's wasting,' Edge said. 'And knowing you've got to catch

60

up with me will maybe hurry you some. Changing their minds ain't all that women are noted for.'

He swung up into the saddle on the livery stable threshold.

'How about the nag for fifty, Miss Diamond?' Florin urged.

'No reflection upon your parents, Mr Edge!' Emma said harshly. 'But you are what Mr Florin called you.'

'Gelding's worth twenty at the most,' Edge said evenly as he heeled his horse into the wind.

'You're right, Miss Diamond!' Florin snarled, stuffing a twenty into his apron pocket and offering Emma the other two bills. 'And he's a mean one, too.'

Chapter Six

EDGE sensed watching eyes as he rode north along Lone Star Street and then swung the gelding on to the Pecos Trail. But there was no allied feeling of being in danger. Perhaps many citizens of Dream Creek were following his progress until he made the turn on to the open trail and was lost to sight beyond the slaughter-house: but something more than a hunch told him that one secret observer would be the sullen lawman.

Few lights were burning in town: and even fewer winked at him across the grazing land to pinpoint the position of the scattered sheep farms. But nature showed the lone rider the country spread out ahead of him: a pale half-moon shedding a diffused glow through a high layer of scudding white clouds. It was low foothill country, the land folding rather than rearing up to the north; and falling gently down to the river in the south. Most of it covered with short grass. But there was plenty of cover in the shallow dips, among widely spaced stands of timber and behind the occasional rock-sided mesa.

And the tall half-breed's eyes, narrowed against the wind

cutting in from his right, surveyed each possible hiding place with a deceptive nonchalance. This attentiveness to his surroundings was involuntary, for his violence-bred sense of danger lay dormant. Sheriff Schabar, the sole threat from Dream Creek, had watched him leave town and had not followed. Conrad Andrews and the men he rode with were far ahead.

But constant vigilance for the first sign of unexpected attack – too easily maintained to be regarded as fear – had become an unbreakable habit for the man called Edge.

A habit which had begun to be formed six years before he adopted such a clipped name. At the start of a long war when, often, he had to be on his guard against the men he fought with as well as those he fought against. During each battle and skirmish of that war, he had developed and nurtured this ability to the same extent that he built up his fighting skills. And, as much as speed and efficiency with handgun, rifle and the deadly razor, it had enabled him to survive the war.

He had planned then to forget such hard and bloodily learned lessons: to return to the Iowa farm and live at peace like the sheepmen on the quiet homesteads outside Dream Creek. But fate had decreed otherwise. The farm to which he returned was a charred ruin and the invalid brother who had waited so long for him to come back was dead.

War had dehumanised Josiah C. Hedges. The bitter rewards of war had made a dehumanised animal out of Edge. A straying animal who had once sought to put down roots – under the gentle influence of a woman. But fate had again struck a cruel blow. Even more brutal than the first. For he had been able to track down and claim his revenge against the killers of his brother. Although he did not lift a hand against her, he blamed himself for the ghastly death of his wife.

And so now he rode a constant and aimless trail, reluctant and perhaps even afraid to put down roots – or even make the attempt. His sole purpose was to survive, because life was all he possessed. And to lose this would be to submit to the fate that had become the most powerful of all his enemies.

He rode throughout the entire night, low-crowned hat pulled over his forehead and the collar of his black, hip-length jacket turned up around his neck. Even when the wind dropped an hour before dawn, the air stayed bitterly cold. But the clouds had been driven south into Mexico and the half-moon was brighter, its light augmented by a skyful of brilliant stars.

The pocket of good grazing land claimed by the sheepmen was far behind him and the terrain was harsher. Semi-desert country of bare rock, the sand of erosion, and vegetation that was mostly scrub-grass and mesquite.

But the Pecos Trail was still clearly defined, swinging northwards, away from the Rio Grande towards a joining with the San Antonio–El Paso trail. That was what Edge guessed it would do, anyway, from the direction it was taking. And he knew that when the two trails met, he would be on recently familiar territory. For, not many weeks previously, he had ridden out of El Paso, striking eastwards for San Antonio. That had been shortly after he finished a job of work for another woman. The job had panned out badly for both the woman and himself: but he had made a little money and he had survived. He rode eastwards for the simple reason that he left in the afternoon and this direction kept the sun out of his eyes.

Now he was close to back-tracking on himself, cold and as watchful as ever: on the slim chance another woman would make up her mind and hire him – and the even slimmer chance he could recover her dead father's hundred thousand dollars.

But all that mattered was that he was alive and he was moving. The man called Edge never expected, and seldom demanded, more than this. For this was his way. Or the way it had to be.

He made camp in an arroyo under a high bluff as the first light of dawn showed at his back. A clump of mesquite supplied kindling for a fire and the gelding was able to feed and water himself on scrub grass and at a brackish water hole. Edge breakfasted on fried salt pork and coffee.

The sun was clear of the horizon and a distant rider showed as a lone speck beneath its trailing arc when Edge doused the fire's embers and remounted. He moved off along the trail at the same energy-conserving pace he had maintained throughout the hours of darkness. His eyes, narrowed to slits of ice-blue, constantly altered their focus and direction of gaze. And, each time he glanced over his shoulder, the rider behind him was either a little closer or lost to sight beyond an intervening feature of terrain.

'Mr Edge!' Emma Diamond yelled breathlessly, an hour after the half-breed had broken camp. 'Please wait for me!'

He reined his horse to a halt and took off his coat. He draped it over his saddlehorn, unhooked a canteen and drank from it, turning in the saddle to watch her approach. He had heard the hoofbeats of her mount slow from a flat-out gallop just before she shouted the plea. Now, as the gelding approached at a winded walk, the woman brushed frantically at her clothing to rid it of trail dust. Then she used a handkerchief to wipe away the grimy sweat from her face.

Nonetheless, she looked hot, dirty and weary as she drew her gelding to a halt alongside Edge's horse. Anger lurked close to the surface of her green eyes. But she chewed hard on her lower lip and controlled the emotion from exploding.

'You must have seen me when I was miles away, Mr Edge,' she accused, having to suck in some more air after every couple of words.

'Saw somebody,' he allowed, capping the canteen.

She could not conceal the anger from her movements as she snatched up her own canteen. She tried the impossible – to give the act a ladylike air as she sucked thirstily from the canteen's neck.

'So why didn't you wait?' she asked when she had drank her fill. Her breathing was less noisy and more even.

He heeled his horse forward. Emma hurried to cap her canteen and get up alongside Edge again.

'Couldn't be sure it was you,' he told her. 'Knew if it was, you'd catch up.'

She made a low sound deep in her throat. 'You are an insufferable man, Mr Edge!'

'Don't claim to be anything, ma'am,' he answered. 'You get the horse for twenty?'

'Plus the saddle and bridle,' she replied after a lengthy pause during which Edge showed no intention of pursuing the matter.

5   65

'Mr Florin said that if I chose to ride with you, I deserved kindness from other directions.'

The half-breed eyed the sweat-lathered horse and the well-worn gear. He spat on to the trail ahead. 'Guess the horse was only worth fifteen bucks,' he commented sardonically.

'Insufferable!' Emma hissed.

Edge rode in silence. The woman spent five minutes recovering her breath completely, as she did some more cleaning work on her clothes and face. Then:

'Horseback riding in the West is outside my experience, Mr Edge. I took the advice of the storekeepers concerning clothes and supplies.'

Now that most of the dust was removed, her garb showed its newness. High-sided riding boots, tight pants that were tucked into them, a matching jacket with shiny buttons, and a wide-brimmed hat that were all black. A white blouse under the jacket, unfastened to a modest extent two inches below the base of her throat. The clothing pointed up the shabbiness of the saddle and bedroll lashed on behind.

'The Dream Creek tailor knows his job,' Edge acknowledged.

'Do you know your job, Mr Edge?' Emma countered at once.

He showed her a cold grin. 'I have a knack of locating money, ma'am,' he replied. 'And sometimes it even turns up where I happen to be. Like yesterday morning.'

Emma Diamond was not beautiful. Even the handsomeness of her face had more to do with the visible strength of character rather than feminine fairness. When her facial muscles grew tense – as now – she became almost homely.

'I'd prefer to forget about the events of yesterday morning, Mr Edge,' she said firmly.

Edge shook his head. 'I wouldn't do that, if I were you. Not until you get the money back where you figure it belongs. That could take a long time and the going could get rough.'

'And so?'

'And so you might want to give up on the idea – you being a woman liable to change her mind. But if you keep thinking how rough it was when you lost the money . . .'

'Is that what keeps you acting so hard, Mr Edge?' Emma cut in. 'Thinking about the past?'

'Ain't no act, ma'am.'

'You know what I mean!'

'Nothing else to think about. Future hasn't happened and the present is happening right now.'

The woman realised that this was the closest she had ever come to opening a normal conversation with the impassive and taciturn tall man.

'Was the past all bad?' she asked, and anger was absent from her voice now. It held a tone of sympathy.

Edge mistook it for pity. 'The parts I think about!' he rasped.

She snatched a look at his profile and the lean flesh seemed as hard and immobile as the face of the bluff they were passing. She allowed several seconds to slide back into an unharsh past, then:

'Have you seen anything to prove the men came this way?' Her voice was neutral, businesslike.

'Not until now,' he replied, nodding almost imperceptibly to indicate a point two hundred yards along the trail.

An unsaddled horse had wandered out on to the trail from around the end of the bluff. The sun was high enough now to generate a promise of the searing heat it was holding in reserve for the rest of the day. But there was no shimmer yet and the near-empty land and its features showed up in stark clarity.

'A horse?' Emma said. Without scorn, for her dislike of the dark-skinned half-breed did not cloud her respect for his judgement. 'It could be a mustang.'

'Shod,' Edge answered. 'A mare. Old and owned by somebody who doesn't give a damn about horseflesh.'

A look of fear clouded Emma's green eyes. She recalled a phrase Florin had spoken under the threat of the razor: *Tom had his broken down old mare saddled and ready to ride.*

'Shouldn't you get your gun ready, Mr Edge?' she asked, lowering her voice to a whisper as they narrowed the gap on the mare.

'Horse ain't in that bad a shape,' the half-breed replied evenly.

The whisper took on a hissing note. 'You know what I mean! In case they're hiding up there.'

'If they're hiding, I figure they can do better than that, ma'am.'

The mare had remained stationary after rounding the angle of the bluff and seeing the newcomers. As Edge and Emma rode closer, they saw just how badly the animal had been treated. Under-feeding caused the ribs to show in relief against the dappled grey coat. The coat was dull from lack of grooming. The scabs of old sores and the crusted blood of more recent ones showed where the saddle had been cinched too tight, spurs had been dug in and a quirt had been misused.

'Such people have no right to own animals!' Emma accused, foresaking her previous low tones, incensed by the mare's distressed state and gaining confidence from Edge's easy manner.

'This one won't be riding anything else unless it's got wings,' the half-breed responded evenly as he reined his gelding at the end of the bluff.

The mare continued to stand in motionless dejection across the centre of the trail. Emma had to steer her mount around the animal in order to see what lay at the base of the bluff's west-facing cliff.

She started a scream, which faded into a moan. Her body went rigid, and then became limp. As Edge slid from his saddle, she slumped and almost toppled to the ground. But she clung frantically to the saddlehorn, eyes wide and staring. Her mouth flapped several times before she was able to voice the words in her throat.

'Holy Mother of God,' she croaked, but with deep reverence.

'Doubtful a feller like him will get to meet the lady,' Edge muttered, ambling across to the man who was the object of Emma Diamond's horror.

'It's Tom!' she gasped. She made to dismount, swayed, and held her seat in the saddle.

'The bum arm points to it,' Edge growled.

Tom was in his early twenties and would not get to be many hours older.

Crusted blood on the untidy heap of his discarded clothing

68

showed he had been shot before he was stripped. Twice. Once in each ankle to disable him. Then, naked as the day he was born, he had been lashed to a large slab of rock canted to the base of the cliff. Four lengths of rope had been used – below the knees, across the belly, around the chest and upper arms and at the throat. Then they had done something with a knife and ridden off, leaving him exposed to the brutal harshness of the sun on its afternoon crawl down the western dome of the sky.

'His mouth!' Emma gasped. 'What have they done to Tom's mouth?'

The dying youngster had managed to raise his head once when he became aware of people close to him. But then his chin had thudded back down on to the rope around his throat before the half-breed or the woman could see what had caused the broad run of now dry blood which reached from his chest to his genitals.

Edge halted immediately in front of the trapped and tortured man and dropped on to his haunches. Tom's eyelids flickered to show pale green eyes that failed to get a focus on his appraiser before they closed again. Edge glanced into the gaping, blood-blackened mouth and a dozen bloated flies swarmed out. He swatted them lazily away from his stubbled face as he rose and drew the razor.

'Cut out his tongue,' he reported as he leaned towards the mutilated man and began to saw at the restraining ropes.

'How . . . !' Emma started to shriek as she turned her drained face up towards the sky.

The strength went from her hands as she swayed again. She tilted far out to the side and was unable to hold herself in the sadle. She hit the ground hard, the groan of pain revealing that she did not lose consciousness. But she remained limply paralysed with horror as she watched the tall, lean, dark-skinned half-breed complete his chore.

And, despite the muscle-freezing horror that gripped her, she was able to feel surprise at a new facet of the man called Edge which was revealed. A totally unselfconscious gentleness that seemed as natural to him as breathing.

He cut through the lower ropes first. Then, before he put the razor to the bonds at throat and chest, he took the weight of Tom. When the final strand parted, he tossed away the razor so that he had both hands free to lift the injured man and then lower him, full-length, to the dusty ground. Then, almost with the same degree of tenderness of a devoted father taking care of a much-loved child, he gathered up Tom's clothing and formed it into a pillow. But no father in such circumstances would ever wear such an expression of utter impassiveness.

'He's alive?' Emma gasped. She clawed at the ground, trying to get up. But her strength refused to return.

'For a while,' Edge answered, glancing around at the immediate area beneath the bluff, then dropping into a squat at the side of Tom's head. 'Tougher than he looks, but nobody's that tough.'

There had been a camp here. The night wind had scattered a lot of the sign: but a few dark embers of a former fire still showed and there was a crushed cigar butt and two piles of horse droppings close by. A midday stopover, the half-breed guessed. Because Tom's face, chest, belly and thighs were blistered and flaked by long exposure to sun. Perhaps the bitter cold of night had come as a relief – at first.

He had not opened his eyes again, but now he did. There was pain in them, leaving no room to express anything else if he was aware of his helper. His chest had hardly moved at all as he breathed. But abruptly he sucked in deeply through his mucus-blocked nostrils. The sound of it was louder than the croak that caught in his throat. The congealed blood in his mouth made brittle cracking noises as he moved his lips.

'Can't you help him?' Emma begged.

'Beyond it,' Edge muttered. 'But maybe he can do us some good.' He reached for his razor and leaned close to put his mouth close to Tom's ear.

'No!' Emma said shrilly, and tried again to get up on to all fours. She made it, but fell flat when she tried to rise further.

'Where they heading, feller?' Edge asked, pronouncing the words distinctly.

Tom smelled bad, and not only with the odours of congealed blood and approaching death. His mop of curly blond hair was

70

rancid with months-old dirt. He was dehydrated now, but the sweat drawn from him by the merciless sun had dislodged a long build-up of grime from every pore in his lanky body. His bowels and bladder had emptied.

Edge lifted the youngster's right hand and folded the nail-bitten fingers around the razor's wooden handle. It had to be the right. Tom's left hand and arm were a bloodless, skin-puckered, fleshless parody of a human limb. The scaly scar-tissue of an old wound just above the elbow showed where the life-giving nerves and blood-vessels had been irreparably severed.

'I thought you were going to . . . ' Emma started.

Edge continued to ignore her as he reached out and, with extreme gentleness again, tipped Tom on to his left side. The razor slipped from his fingers and Edge replaced it and repeated his question. Over on the trail, Emma hauled herself to her feet and took faltering steps out of the sun's glare into the shade cast by the bluff.

'For you and me both, feller,' Edge urged as the mutilated man opened his eyes once more. 'If you can write, they won't get to spend your share.'

Emma came to stand over Tom and Edge as the injured boy started to use the razor's point to make marks in the dust. She was behind Tom now that he was held on his side by Edge and he was probably unaware of her. Edge ignored her, craning his head around to try to decipher the shaky lines which the razor was inscribing in the dry dust. The writer and the reader both had their eyes cracked to narrow slits of intense concentration.

Emma's new boots creaked as she moved around the two men, to look down in harrowing pity at the blistered and blood-crusted face of Tom.

'E-L-P-A,' Edge muttered, and then the razor fell from the hand which had begun to tremble.

Tom made a sound in his throat like that of a trapped wild animal – but not loud. Edge glanced at his face, which was upturned towards the woman. The pain in his green eyes was more intense than before. And it was not entirely physical, for his punished features showed lines of recognition.

71

Then he made another low sound deep in his throat; his body was abruptly rigid; his eyes snapped closed and then wide open again. When Edge released him, he became limp and rolled on to his face, covering the four letters he had scrawled. There was no further movement.

'He's dead,' Emma whispered as she crossed herself.

Edge raised the body a little to retrieve the razor and return it to the neck pouch. He stood up.

'He looked at me and he died,' the woman said.

'Maybe it's the new clothes,' the half-breed growled as he went to his horse.

'What?' Emma asked absently, continuing to stare down at the dead body.

Edge raked his hooded eyes over the tight-fitting riding habit that contoured the slender curves of her body. 'You sure look dressed to kill,' he muttered.

Chapter Seven

'TOM was my brother,' Emma said out of the depth of her sadness as she stirred a skillet of frying beans.

It was the first time she had spoken since she glared contemptuously at Edge in the shadow of the bluff when he told her the buzzards would take care of the youngster's remains. She had refused to allow this to happen and had gathered enough scattered rocks to stack into a funeral pile atop the body. It took a long time and Edge did nothing except wait for her until the work was finished and she had knelt in prayer beside the rocks.

They had ridden in silence until early afternoon, when the half-breed called a halt at an abandoned stage line shack with a well outside. She had shaken her head at his tacit offer of food, then walked off into a cypress grove while he made a meal of canned meat and tepid water.

When she returned from the grove, her face was puffy from tears. In such distress, she was at her most attractive. But then she washed up and, when they remounted to ride for the junction with the main east–west trail, she wore the familiar façade of strong determination and self-reliance. Then, as the heat built up and the surrounding horizons shimmered in closer, her physical discomfort acted to trigger her true emotions into penetrating the false front.

It was as if she needed all her strength of character to match the slow but unrelenting pace of the man: to an extent that she was unable to spare any for a false front. The beads of sweat standing out on her sun-reddened cheeks encouraged the held-back tears to squeeze from the corners of her screwed-up eyes.

And for the first time, she welcomed the utterly cold lack of compassion in Edge. For, had he offered to halt awhile, or even showed her a sympathetic glance, such a gesture would have opened the floodgates on the full weight of her feelings. And Tom did not deserve such grief.

'It showed in the eyes,' the half-breed said as he sat down beside the fire after hobbling the two geldings. 'Not just the colour. And the bone structures of the faces were alike.'

The camp site was at the side of the main trail, half-a-dozen miles towards El Paso from where they had joined it. In a narrow ravine with a clear stream running down one side. There was sweet grass to feed the horses, and a tangle of brush between the trunks of some stunted pine trees which would provide a wind-break if the norther came again tonight. It was after sundown and almost completely dark when Edge decided to stop in the ravine. And still the woman failed to open a conversation. While Edge had built a fire and then attended to the horses, she had unpacked her saddlebags and started to prepare a meal.

'You didn't know until you saw him?' Her misery was great, but it was now deeply buried inside her. In the cool of evening after a long day's ride under a hot sun, her face looked glowing and healthy in the dancing firelight. Her eyes gleamed in reflection and her teeth showed very white between the full lips.

'I figured you recognised the bum arm bit when you heard about him,' Edge answered, rasping the back of a hand over his stubbled jaw.

She acknowledged this with a nod as she continued to stir the

74

cooking food. 'My father was quite mad, of course,' she said in her flat, emotionless voice. 'It was Tom who drove him into insanity. He was always the favourite child, even though our mother died giving birth to him.' She shrugged. 'Or perhaps because of that. But Tom was wild, Mr Edge. He led a wild life.'

'He died pretty wild, too,' the half-breed muttered, testing the extent of the woman's changed mood.

But she ignored the comment, and belied her apparent vagueness. She removed the beans to the side of the fire before they could burn, and then attended to the meat.

'He became an outlaw. Alone at first, robbing stages and stores. But then he got shot in the arm while he was trying to rob an elderly couple of their life savings. It was a bad wound that made his left arm and hand useless. And he was left-handed.

'But it didn't change his ways. He could not work alone any more, so he joined a gang. Then another and another. He wasn't very old, Mr Edge. Twenty-three, but he'd done a lot of wicked things.'

'Younger fellers work faster,' Edge commented, and was again ignored – except as a captive listener.

'Our father grew gradually more disenchanted with Tom and his ways. And, when he heard Tom had been sent to the penitentiary for murder, he withdrew into insanity. Then Tom escaped with some other men and he came to Chicago to ask for money. He had never done that before. Father refused and there was a fight. Tom ran and Father lived just long enough for me to get to him and hear his last requests.'

She distributed the food between two plates and looked hard at Edge as she handed him his meal.

'I've been mourning Tom as he was when he was a child,' she said stiffly. 'And I'd cry for my worst enemy if he died like that. I choose to recall the good parts of the past, I suppose.'

'Did you hear me complaining, ma'am?' Edge asked.

She showed irritation. 'You never ask any questions!' she accused. 'And there are times when everybody needs to talk.'

'Guess I'm different to everybody.'

75

'You most certainly are!' she responded, still flaring a little. Then her emotions calmed as he began to eat. Her voice became flat again. 'I suppose Father must have taunted Tom with what he intended to do with his money. Tom was waiting for me in Dream Creek, so he must have.'

'It figures,' Edge agreed. 'It also figures he didn't trust himself to handle the job alone.'

'And there was a falling out?' Emma suggested. 'Perhaps when they divided the money between them.'

'Your brother fell real hard.'

Silence came between them again, as they squatted on opposite sides of the fire, eating the evening meal. But there was no longer any hint of tension in the absence of words. The crackling of the burning firewood could have been the sounds of the barrier as it was constantly broken down and kept open for further communication.

'You would never kill a man like that, would you, Mr Edge?' Emma asked after she had washed the dirty pots and plates and poured two mugs of steaming coffee.

The half-breed spat into the fire, aware of the grimace this provoked on the woman's face.

'You do nothing to encourage people to like you, do you?' She showed sadness again, but not for her dead brother and the manner of his dying. 'And I think I know why.'

'And I think you're going to tell me what you think,' Edge said softly.

'Because you're afraid. Afraid of human relationships that go beneath the most shallow of levels. And I think that's terrible.'

She waited for a response. Even grew physically tense in expectation of a barbed vocal attack.

'Thinking's free, ma'am,' Edge replied evenly, setting down his mug to roll a cigarette. 'Like speech.'

'Not always. It cost Barney Castle a cut lip that would have scarred him for life if he had lived.'

'That was the idea,' Edge told her. 'Every time he opened his mouth he would have felt that cut. And if he'd had any sense, he would have thought about what he was going to say. It could have saved his life – if he'd had any sense.'

76

'No,' Emma said pensively.

'It was the idea,' Edge countered again. 'But it just didn't work on the kid.'

'I mean, no, you'd never kill a man the way my brother was killed. You have to be all bad to do that. And you're not all bad, Mr Edge.'

'If ever I need a character reference, ma'am, I'll know who to –'

'Like just taking the fifty dollars from Mr Florin,' Emma cut in. 'Oh, I know it had nothing to do with easing his conscience. But you decided it would be poetic justice for the gang's own money to be used to catch up with them. You only took the fifty though.'

Edge drew hard against the cigarette.

'With ten grand coming, I could afford to be generous.'

Emma threw up her hands in a gesture of surrender. 'All right, Mr Edge. I'm foolish to keep talking like this. You don't need to be liked or even understood. And since we will certainly never see each other again when this is over, there is no reason why I have to like or understand you. I will therefore keep my thoughts to myself.'

The half-breed held his peace as he smoked the cigarette and drank the coffee. Then he unfastened his bedroll and spread it.

'You're going to sleep already?' Emma asked. 'But it's so early.'

'Makes it easier to get up early,' Edge answered as he drew off his boots.

'I won't be able to sleep after what has happened.'

Edge put his Winchester to one side of the spread bedding and his gunbelt on the other, with the butt of the holstered Colt jutting up for ease of access.

'Maybe you will later,' he replied. 'When you get tired of talking.'

He got under the blanket, rested the back of his head on his saddle and tipped his hat forward over his face.

'It takes two to –'

'Dance, like a lot of other things. And I ain't in the mood for dancing or talking right now. You have anything else in mind, ma'am?'

'Insufferable!' Emma exploded, and snatched up the dirty coffee mugs to wash them. Then she bedded down, taking off only her boots and hat. She ended another long silence, talking with low-voiced anger, as if to herself. 'I don't know why we have to make such an early start, anyway. We can't even be sure the men came – '

'E-L-P-A,' Edge recited from under his hat.

'What?'

'Your brother figured they were heading for El Paso.'

She sighed. 'Oh, you're so smart!' she rasped, making it sound like an insult.

'It's getting a full night's rest that does it,' he muttered sardonically. 'And keeping my mind on my job.'

'Don't you think my mind – '

'Ain't your mind that's trying to get on my mind, ma'am.'

'Oh, you beast!' she exclaimed. 'You mean my body!'

She lapsed into silence after that, recalling the horror of the assault on her. And, after awhile, the regular breathing of the sleeping man had a lulling effect on the turmoil of memories in her mind. She slid into her own kind of, much deeper, sleep.

It took a further three days for them to reach El Paso and, during the entire time, Emma Diamond made a conscious effort to speak only when it was strictly necessary. And, particularly at night camp, she went out of her way not to be provocative. They reached the adobe-built, dusty town in the early evening and, as they dismounted in front of the Bella Cantina in the Mexican quarter, she touched his arm.

'Thank you, Mr Edge,' she said.

'What did I do?' he asked.

'Nothing, and you know what I mean. Thank you for that.'

'Can't say it was a pleasure, ma'am,' the half-breed rasped. 'But we could have a long way to go still.'

She didn't get angry as he eased the Winchester from the saddleboot and turned towards the lamplit, arched entrance of the cantina. 'I have a very good reason for denying you that pleasure, Mr Edge,' she said as she hurried to join him inside,

78

casting apprehensive glances at the men, out on the street and inside the building, who were eyeing her with unconcealed sexual interest. 'But I prefer to keep it to myself.'

'I noticed that,' Edge said evenly, and nodded to a nervously smiling Mexican behind the short length of bar.

'Hi, *señor*,' the bartender greeted.

'Yeah, it sure smells that way,' Edge rasped. 'But the lady and I'd still like a room here.'

The Mexican, who was middle-aged and had a squint, failed to understand the criticism of the cantina. Perhaps he had worked there so long he failed to notice the smell of the place any more. The atmosphere was fetid with dirt, greasy cooking, spilled liquor, cheap tobacco and unwashed bodies. Two lamps burned on low wicks, as if to conceal most of what caused the bad odours.

'A room you may certainly have, *señor*,' the squint-eyed man offered. 'But you should know that elsewhere in El Paso there are places more suitable for the *Americano señora*.'

'I think there has to be, Mr Edge,' Emma whispered after raking her nervous eyes around the small, hot cantina. There were a dozen men drinking in the place. Two young Americans and the remainder Mexicans, spanning a twenty to seventy age scale. Their expressions as she clashed eyes with each man ranged from wistful to lip-licking lust. 'I'm not going to like it here.'

'But I figure she's gonna get it here, Luke,' the red-headed young American said with a laugh, his voice purposely loud.

'Reckon so, Johnnie,' his stockily built companion replied in the same amused tone. 'Specially since she ain't his *señora*, on account she calls him mister.'

'The room?' Edge asked the bartender.

The Mexican shrugged and reached for a row of four keys hung beneath a shelf behind him. 'One dollar, *señor*. All I claim for my place is that she is cheap.'

'Reckon he's gotta make the same claim about her, Luke!' Johnnie taunted. When he spoke fast, the liquor could be heard in his voice: causing it to slur.

Emma had grabbed hold of Edge's upper arm again. She felt

the flesh become taut beneath her fingers. 'They're drunk!' she whispered tensely. 'Let's get to the room or go to another place. Please?'

'*Si señor,*' the suddenly frightened man behind the bar urged. 'I think one thing or the other would be wise.'

He stared hard at the half-breed's face and, despite the low level of light, he saw the ice-cold anger in the glittering eyes and hovering at the abruptly tightened mouthline. He mouthed an obscenity in his own language and moved sideways along the bar.

'Back off, ma'am,' Edge told Emma.

The woman did not have to look so long and hard at the half-breed. For she was familiar with this facet of the man called Edge. Barney Castle had died when she had last seen it. 'Please don't,' she begged, but she released her hold on him and side-stepped along the bar.

Chairlegs scraped on the dirt floor and footfalls thudded as the Mexicans who had been in the centre of the cantina hurried to get to the sides.

'You want to apologise to Miss Diamond, feller?' Edge asked.

'I don't like talkin' to a guy's back, mister!' Johnnie snarled.

The Winchester was still canted to Edge's shoulder. He lowered it a little, to rest the stock on the bartop. When it was held rigid, he worked the action. The friction of metal against metal sounded very loud. The noise of El Paso beyond the arched doorway seemed to come from a great distance.

'Johnnie was just funnin', mister!' Luke excused. He could carry his liquor better than his drinking companion. He was clear-eyed enough to see the expressions of dread on the faces of the squinty Mexican and the woman. And clear-headed enough to realise what they meant.

'But I can get real serious!' Johnnie added harshly.

'Maybe even dead serious, feller. Apologise to the lady.'

As he spoke, his voice incongruously even in the tension-riddled atmosphere of the malodorous cantina, he turned to face the man who was taunting him. Slowly, but keyed-up to power into a whirl.

'I sure am sorry, lady,' Luke said quickly, rising from his chair and almost stumbling in his haste to leave the table.

Johnnie rose, too. But his pace was as measured as Edge's had been. The table was just inside the entrance, to the right. He stepped away from it, facing the half-breed across three deserted tables. As if the scene had been carefully stage-managed, both men were standing in the cones of light from the ceiling-hung lamps. The flickering illumination showed Johnnie to be about twenty-five: well-dressed and freshly washed-up and shaved for a night on the town. Two holstered guns hung from his expensive-looking belt. And he held his manicured hands in position for a fast draw.

'She's here, so she ain't no lady!' he rasped. He had shrugged off the effects of the liquor now. But if he regretted starting the trouble, he showed no outward sign of it. He looked across at the taller, leaner man with a cool, steady stare.

'Please settle this matter outside, *señors*,' the man behind the bar pleaded.

'Matter's settled,' Edge replied thoughtfully. 'This lady's a lady. Only one loose end to tie up.'

'*Señor?*'

'Don't kill him, Mr Edge!' Emma begged.

The half-breed turned his head to the side – away from the woman. And spat. 'Do it your way, ma'am,' he said.

Then his head snapped to face front. The Winchester whipped down to slap into the cupped palm of his free hand.

'Oh, Christ!' Luke yelled.

Emma threw up her hands to cover her face.

Johnnie drew his matched Navy Colts.

The Winchester exploded and Johnnie screamed. His fingers squeezed the triggers of both revolvers. But the bullets spewed by the barrels angled up at the ceiling as the man was hurled backwards. Then the guns dropped from his hands as he crashed full-length across a table top, sending a bottle and two glasses crashing in the wake of the guns. A great splash of blood appeared at the crotch of his pants and spread down his thighs and across the shirt that was taut over his belly.

Luke made to move towards the injured man, but then froze as Edge worked the action of the rifle and started forward.

Whispered conversations were virtually still-born as all eyes followed the unhurried progress of the half-breed. Johnnie slid to the floor and did not move. But a low whimpering from his bloodless lips evidenced that he was still conscious. And the cone of light from the overhead lamp showed the defiance shining through the pain in his eyes as he stared up at the towering figure of Edge.

'She ain't no friggin' lady, mister!' he croaked.

'Johnnie, you're askin' to get killed!' Luke warned hoarsely.

Edge pursed his lips and glanced at the still-expanding blood stain with the bubbling hole at its centre. 'Figure that's just what he's doing,' he muttered. 'But I got all I need from him.'

'I ain't sayin' I'm sorry, you bas – ' He groaned as a fresh wave of pain hit him. He gritted his teeth. 'She's no more a lady than I am.'

Edge canted the rifle to his shoulder and eased the hammer to the rest. 'You don't have to say anything, feller. I can see what I wanted.'

'See what, *señor*?' the squint-eyed owner of the cantina asked in confusion as the half-breed returned to the bar and picked up the room key.

'All a matter of sex,' Edge replied lightly as he nodded for the trembling Emma Diamond to go ahead of him through a doorway into the back of the place. 'Wanted an apology for the lady. Got an apology for a man.'

Chapter Eight

THE Bella Cantina was a single-storey building with adobe outer walls, a dirt floor and a roof of timber. The sleeping accommodation behind the bar-room was formed into separate rooms by canvas partitions. There was no way to block the room entrances and inside each there was a large cot covered with straw and a blanket. Nothing else. Light was from the moon shafting in through a small, glassless window. The smell of old patrons clung to the rooms. The fresher odours of the bar-room filtered through into the back of the cantina.

'It's disgusting and it's filthy,' Emma gasped. 'And there is only one bed.'

'Yeah,' Edge agreed curtly, and sat on the blanket-covered straw of the bed. Cockroaches made scuttling noises as they got out from under him.

'So what are we doing here?' she demanded. She was standing at the window, staring out into the alley that ran behind the building, allowing the last grains of tension to drain out of her.

But suddenly she spun around. 'You didn't really intend that we should – '

'I didn't and I don't!' he cut in coldly. 'You're a lady, lady. I figured I made that point pretty plain out there just now. Same way you've made it plain my pay's going to be in dollars and nothing more.'

'Well, in this pigsty it seems you can only work for one thing!' She stared distastefully at the evil-smelling bed.

Edge rose with a sigh and began to amble about in the restricted space. Emma softened her expression and her voice.

'I'm sorry, Mr Edge. But you saw what happened to me when that man . . . And I'm not very familiar with men . . . '

'You can say that again,' the half-breed muttered.

'But if you'd only tell me what you plan to do, then I wouldn't keep thinking the worst.'

He resumed his seat on the bed and rolled a cigarette. The tobacco smoke did something to mute the stench of the room.

'Are we going to stay here all night?' she asked, a little shrilly.

'We're waiting, is all.'

'For what?'

'The local lawman.'

'That's something, at least,' she said with a sigh. 'What then? I have a right to know. After all, I am paying – '

'No law against the lady putting up the cash,' a man said from the open entrance of the room. 'And I ain't no prude personally. But shootin' folks is something different.'

As he stepped into the room, the moonlight from the window struck his badge of office and his eyes. The eyes looked harder than the metal of the star.

'The other man started it, Sheriff!' Emma defended.

There was something lazy about the lawman, who was tall and broadly built and wore clothes that seemed a couple of sizes too small for him. The tight-stretched fabric of his pants and shirt contoured a lot of muscle. He seemed on the point of leaning against the wall, then realised the canvas would not support him.

He touched the brim of his plainsman's hat. 'There's a dozen eye-witnesses to back that up, ma'am,' he drawled. 'Including Luke Danvers. Self-defence right enough. But I still think that sassy Johnnie Cash got hit in a mighty bad place.'

'Johnnie Cash?' Edge asked.

'That's his name.'

'Didn't his Ma tell him not to bring his guns to town?'

'Forget him, mister!' the sheriff said, hardening his tone. 'I have. Just here to tell you El Paso's got its fair share of troubles and don't want no more. You shoot anyone else and I won't forget it.' He tapped the butt of the revolver in his holster. 'And this ain't the only law gun hereabouts.'

Edge nodded. 'We're in the same business, Sheriff.'

The man in the doorway shook his head. 'You're no lawman, Edge.'

'But I'm looking for troublemakers. Six of them.'

Now the sheriff nodded. 'Bounty-hunter, uh?'

'He is working for me, Sheriff,' Emma said. 'We are seeking some men who –'

'Looking for Conrad Andrews and his bunch,' the half-breed supplied. 'They got something belongs to the talkative lady.'

'Insufferable!' Emma snorted softly.

The lawman clicked his tongue against the roof of his mouth. 'Something like money, uh?'

'A lot like it, feller. And a lot of it.'

The big man in the doorway sighed. 'They're sure spending it like there's no tomorrow.'

'Then they are in El Paso?' Emma exclaimed excitedly.

'Staying at a better place than this, ma'am.' He glanced around the room, seemed set to spit, then looked at Emma and decided against it.

'Which is why we're in a place like this,' Edge supplied.

'They know you?'

'The lady,' Edge replied. 'They saw a lot of her.'

Emma picked up the double-meaning and glared at Edge. But he was concentrating on the sheriff. So she turned her anger on the lawman. 'You must know they're criminals! Why haven't you arrested them?'

'El Paso's my patch, ma'am. I got a stack of wanted bills on

Andrews, Harry and George Hare, Kenyon Lamb, Ira Walker and the Jap. But that's other folks business. They ain't even spit on the sidewalk in my patch, far as I know.'

'That is a terrible attitude to take!' Emma accused, and glared fleetingly at Edge again. 'I have come to expect it from some kinds of men. But you are a peace officer, Sheriff!'

'That sure is my job, ma'am,' he agreed. 'Keepin' the peace. But them six outlaws stick closer together than bees around a honeypot. And if me and my deputies try to take them . . . well, be like full-scale war instead of peace. Course, if they started in with their bad ways, then that'd be a different matter. Be them startin' the war on my patch.' He swung his gaze towards the still seated Edge as the half-breed ground out the cigarette under his heel. 'And I ain't just talkin' for benefit of the lady, Edge?'

'I been listening, too, feller,' the half-breed responded.

A nod and an easy smile. 'Then my visit ain't been wasted. You got my message. If you figure to tangle with Andrews and his bunch – and I figure you fully intend to – then you do it off my patch, mister.' He touched his hat brim. 'Ma'am,' he said, and moved away as quietly as he had approached.

'I think it is disgusting!' Emma said, her voice little short of a snarl. 'A peace officer who allows wanted criminals to roam freely, spending their stolen money.'

'Yeah,' Edge rasped. 'Insufferable. Let's go.'

'Where?'

'Out of here.' He stood up from the bed and canted the rifle to his shoulder.

'Oh, you are so close mouthed!' she snapped.

'But you open yours enough for the two of us, ma'am,' he called back as he went out through the gap in the canvas wall.

Emma held back for a moment, but then the cockroaches made more scuttling sounds in the straw of the bed and she half ran to catch up with Edge.

The cantina was doing brisker business than before. A crush of men – all Mexicans – were drinking and talking about the recent shooting. A lone woman was at the table to the right of the door, scrubbing it clean of blood. All talk was curtailed as Edge and Emma emerged from the back. As the half-breed

86

placed a dollar bill on the bartop, he spoke in the native language of the apprehensive audience.

'Before anyone says anything about a short time, you should know I speak better Mexican than my father – and he was Mexican.'

'You are leaving, *señor*?' the squint-eyed owner of the cantina asked. 'For good?'

'For the lady's good, feller.'

He headed for the door and Emma moved quickly to stay with him in the corridor opened up by the drinkers.

'I almost forget, *señor*. The sheriff, he had a message for you. He say best in Mexico, *señor*. But you have to start at Holden House on Division Street.'

Their horses were still hitched to the rail outside the Bella Cantina, as hungry and weary as the two riders. There were men on the street, perhaps the same ones as before or perhaps different. Whichever, news of the shooting had been circulated and the interest shown in Emma Diamond was curious rather than sensuous.

'I suppose that makes the sheriff here somewhat better than Mr Schabar in Dream Creek,' the woman said as she imitated Edge by swinging up into the saddle. 'At least he is not being obstructive.'

'Both equally as good, I'd say,' Edge answered as he backed the gelding away from the rail and headed him south along the street.

Emma hastened to get alongside him. 'Good?'

'At minding their own business, which is protecting their towns.'

'By detaching themselves from everything that happens outside!' she countered haughtily.

'Schabar didn't want the Andrews bunch back in Dream Creek. The feller here wants them out of El Paso. Ain't nothing wrong with that, ma'am.'

'Because it justifies the existence of a man like you, I suppose? So that you can earn ten thousand dollars doing the work which peace officers choose to neglect.'

The Bella Cantina had been on the south side of town and

already Edge and Emma had ridden clear of El Paso into the sand and sandstone country spread along the northern bank of the Rio Grande.

'You accepted the terms, ma'am,' he reminded her coldly.

'Because I had no alternative, Mr Edge. And that is driven home almost every hour that passes.'

'So what's the hassle?'

'I'm just talking to keep from screaming! With frustration!'

'You only have to ask, ma'am.'

She caught the new tone in his voice and snapped her head around to stare at him. When she saw his easy grin, her eyes generated a glare. 'Even if I could and you were the last man on earth . . . ' Her violence-shocked mind in her weary body ran out of words.

'I'm whittling them down, ma'am,' the half-breed said pensively. 'But if you can't – well, I guess ten thousand is enough compensation.'

'It'll buy a lot of whores,' Emma rasped bitterly.

Edge released the reins and swung both arms. His right hand, reaching across the front of his body, fastened on her shoulder. She had time to shriek a cry of alarm. Then his left back-handed her across the cheek. His grip on her ensured she felt the full weight of the blow – and prevented it knocking her from the horse.

'You brutal beast!' she screamed at him as he calmly resumed a hold on the reins and she streaked a hand to massage the source of her pain. 'You . . . you animal!'

'I'll kill for it, lady,' the half-breed rasped. 'I'll fight for it. I'll work for it. I'll be polite for it. Once I even married for it. But I'll never pay for it.'

'All right!' she snapped. 'All right! You've made it perfectly clear. I'm sorry.'

'There's a way you won't have to keep saying that, ma'am,' Edge told her, his tone soft and even again.

'It doesn't hurt to say it.'

'So why d'you keep rubbing your face?'

She snatched her hand away from her cheek. Moonlight showed the red puffiness against the suntan.

'Just keep your mouth shut as tight as your legs.'

She continued to stare straight ahead, and merely tightened her mouthline in response to the crudeness of the half-breed. And the ride became as silent as it had been a few days earlier after she had buried her wayward brother. Just her mood was different. Then she had been wrapped in the silence of grief. Now she was sulkily sullen.

Edge was as impassively alert as ever as they rode south to the river. Emma submitted in docile silence to having a lead rope hitched to her gelding, so that the half-breed could move ahead and guide her across the Rio Grande. The water was many feet below flood and the two horses were required to swim only a few yards across mid-stream. At either side of this, the geldings could wade, struggling against the currents and dragging their hooves through the sucking mud.

'We're in Mexico now?' Emma said dully as the horses carried them out of the river on the south bank. 'If that doesn't get me another beating?'

'We're in Mexico,' Edge answered.

She glanced to the left and right and ahead. At a barren desert plain and the rearing ruggedness of the Sierra Madre far to the west.

'Why should they come here?' she asked, wearily heeling her horse into a slow walk in the wake of the tall half-breed.

He glanced over his shoulder at her and showed his teeth in a tight grin. 'You'll feel better after a good night's rest, ma'am.'

'But no smarter. Not in your way.'

'Which is why I'm worth ten grand to you.'

'It's worth it to me – just not to be in any way like you, Mr Edge.'

'It's the difference that could have made it interesting,' he told her pointedly, which brought another long silence from Emma Diamond.

Which did not end until they looked down from the crest of a hill at the first sign of human life they had seen since leaving El Paso. It was a Mexican dirt farm – a crude house and ramshackle stable set in a pocket of arable earth surrounded on all sides by almost barren rock. A well at the side of the house showed how the farmer was able to eke a living from the lemon grove and corn field that were the extent of his farm.

'Do you think there is a chance we may rest down there, Mr Edge?' Emma asked flatly.

The half-breed did not reply, and when she dragged her tired gaze away from the farm to look at him, she saw he was examining the scene below with cold suspicion.

'It's just a homestead, surely?' she said. 'Owned by poor peons doing the best they can to stay alive.'

'Poor peons don't ever get to ride good-looking saddle horses,' the half-breed told her, not breaking his concentrated appraisal of the farm and the intervening ground. 'Stay here.'

She swallowed hard and peered down the slope to survey the scene in its new, frightening aspect. 'What if . . . ?'

'Ride for El Paso like you had the Jap breathing down your neck, ma'am. And go home or get yourself another man.'

She looked at him pleadingly. 'I'd rather come with you, Mr Edge.'

He showed her the faintest of sardonic grins. 'Wrong time and place to see if we could make it. Stay here!'

He heeled the gelding off the hilltop and down the gentle incline, listening for the sounds that would indicate Emma Diamond was following him. All he heard was a single, soft-spoken word.

'Insufferable!'

He ignored her.

Cactus plants grew at widely spaced intervals in hollows of sandy earth over the slope. But they offered no cover to anything larger than a lizard. So Edge maintained a direct course towards the farm buildings, riding slow and easy. The gelding's hooves clopped monotonously against the hard rock.

The moon showed the house and stable in stark contrasts of white adobe and black shadow. A window at each side of the house door spilled lamplight, its yellow glow giving a gloss to the coats of the trio of saddled horses hitched to the shaft of a two-wheeled cart canted over on to a broken wheel.

Inside the stable, a burro whinnied. The horses raised their heads and pricked their ears. For a moment they held a frozen posture as they watched the lone rider approaching. Then they dipped their heads again, to munch at the patch of grass growing under the wreck of the cart. In the stable, the burro kicked at the wall.

There were no sounds from inside the house and no one moved across the lighted windows. The chimney of the squat, one-storey building did not smoke. The ripening lemons gave a tangy smell to the hot, dry air immediately around the farm buildings. It was stronger than the atmosphere of disillusion and decay that was a less tangible emanation from the place.

'You will come no closer, *gringo*!'

'Unless you wish to meet your maker, Americano.'

The first man spoke in heavily accented English. The second in Spanish. As they moved to frame themselves in the windows, the door swung open and a third man stepped on to the threshold. All held levelled revolvers and Edge had been allowed to close on the house to within thirty feet. It was long range for handguns, unless the men were either very good or very lucky.

'Only the good die young, so they say,' Edge said, speaking in his father's language, as he reined the gelding to a halt.

The man in the doorway laughed. 'They talk out of a hole not meant to speak through, *señor*. I did not kill a man until I was thirty years. Nor steal a single pesos.'

'And Pedro lives,' the man on the right said enthusiastically.

'Not good, but well,' the English speaker added, and laughed as loudly as Pedro until the obvious leader of the trio snarled a curse at him.

Pedro looked to be about twice the age he had been when he turned bad. His partners were not yet half his age. All were as filthy and unshaven as Edge, but a lot shorter and a great deal thicker around the waist and chest. They were dressed in expensive boots, pants, shirts and hats. American style. All wore crossed bandoliers.

'What you want here, *ombre*?' Pedro demanded, trying out his own English. All humour was gone now. 'You bounty hunting for the damn Federales, uh?'

'Didn't know the heat was on for them,' the half-breed answered in the same language.

Pedro asked a question of the man on the left. He called him Espada. Espada told the top man that the American was trying to be funny.

'*Pulque!*' the man in the doorway snarled, and reached his free hand out of sight beyond the frame. There was a shuffling sound. When his hand swung back into sight, it was fisted around the neck of a bottle. He lashed a foot to the side and the kick exploded a cry of pain. It sounded like an old man. 'I will tell you something, Americano,' Pedro called to Edge. 'I do not think you are funny.' He grinned as he raised the bottle. 'But perhaps my sense of humour will improve when I have some more pulque in my belly. Then, perhaps, I will not shoot you. But, perhaps . . . '

He let the sentence hang and tilted the bottle to his lips. He had to crane his neck backwards and his gaze swept up towards the cloudless sky. But Espada and the other man continued to cover the half-breed with their eyes and long-barrelled Colts.

Edge remained in a nonchalant attitude astride the unmoving gelding, feet still slotted into the stirrups and hands, holding the reins in a loose grip, folded around the saddlehorn. The liquor made gurgling sounds as it flooded down the throat of Pedro.

'Mr Edge!'

The half-breed cursed, kicked his feet free of the stirrups and tipped himself backwards off the horse. Two shots exploded as he took a double-handed grip on the Winchester stock and jerked the rifle from its boot.

Both bullets went high over his upswinging legs, the Mexicans at the windows distracted by Emma Diamond's shout and the beat of hooves as she urged her gelding into a gallop.

'A woman!' Pedro yelled, and dragged the bottle from his lips to smash it against the doorframe.

'Americano!'

'Young!'

The other two gunmen chorused their excited cries. Then all three blasted at the cart as Edge lunged towards it and dived full-length to the ground in its cover. He had turned a full somersault in powering off the back of the gelding – as the horse reared and then bolted in response to the sudden action. He hit the ground with his feet, adjusted his balance, and snarled another curse as he went into a crouch and scrambled for cover.

Splinters of wood spat at his head and one of the hitched horses snorted and rolled over, blood pumping from its holed throat. The bulging eyes stared hatefully at Edge, as if the animal had horsesense enough to blame the stranger for its imminent death.

'I feel the same way about her,' Edge rasped, ducking his head as a further fusillade of three shots cracked into the cart and exploded more splinters.

He glanced up the slope in time to see the woman try to swing the galloping gelding into a tight turn. But the speed was too fast and the slope too steep. The horse lost his footing and tumbled into a roll. Emma was luckier than she deserved to be. Both her feet slid from the stirrups and she had the sense to release her hold on the reins. Horse and rider slammed to the ground, but Emma was several feet away from where the weight of the animal hit. The gelding screamed the agony of a broken back as it quivered and tried to rise. The woman tumbled countless times, giving no sound. She came to rest and was still.

'What is happening?'

Another woman – much older – shouting the terrified demand from inside the house. In Spanish.

'Be quiet, hag!'

From Pedro, and punctuated with three shots. Two bullets smacked into the carcase of the dead horse. The other chipped wood from the rear of the cart and bit into the slope beyond. The two surviving horses of the Mexicans tried to drag the cart in their panic. But the weight of the dead one was too much to move. Edge's gelding had ended his bolt in the lemon grove.

'You think he is dead, Pedro?' Espada asked.

'The crazy woman looks it!' Pedro snarled, 'What a waste!'

Emma's gelding gave a final cry of agony, and died. Silence descended upon the farm and its surrounding country as if it had a physical presence. Edge put his eye to a knot-hole in the side of the cart. Light continued to fall from the two glassless windows and the open doorway. There were no forms to inter-rupt it now. Voices began to hiss in urgent whispers. Edge eased back the hammer of the Winchester, which already had a shell in the breach.

'Hey, *gringo*!' Espada called. 'If you still alive, you listen. Gonna toss the owner of this place out through the door. You toss away your rifle and your pistol, you hear. You don't, by the time I count three, this *ombre* gets shot real bad. If you dead, he gets shot anyway, I guess. Is tough on him but –'

'Don't make a damn speech!' Pedro snarled in Spanish.

He gave a grunt and a man groaned. A woman screamed. The light from the doorway was fleetingly interrupted. A man, dressed in an ankle-length nightshirt, was shoved out into the night. He could do nothing to break his slam into the hard-packed dirt of the yard. For his legs were tied together and his hands were bound behind his back. The impact of the fall knocked the breath from his body. But he sucked in more air and used it to power the words of a prayer.

'One, Americano!' Espada called.

'Two, *gringo*!'

He remained in the motionless crouch, Winchester tightly gripped and eye against the knot hole.

'Three, *bastardo*!'

It was his life against that of a peon who he didn't even know. And the old man in the nightshirt was on borrowed time already. He did not even blink the narrowed eye at the knot hole when a volley of fast shots exploded through the doorway. Simply widened it a fraction, in surprise. For the half-dozen bullets did not even graze the cringing old man as he rolled himself up into a ball – divots of dirt and puffs of dust springing up around him.

'Manuel!' the woman inside the house shrieked.

'Is OK, hag,' Espada announced. 'If we kill your husband, who cook for us, eh? You sure can't.'

He laughed.

The old man in the nightshirt sobbed.

Halfway up the slope in front of the house, Emma Diamond

94

caught her breath and was certain the man called Edge was dead. It was not that she thought him incapable of sacrificing the peon's life for a chance to save his own. She understood too well his philosophy of self-preservation at all costs to think this.

But, she was gripped by the terrifying thought, no man could remain so totally still for so long unless he were dead – or at best, unconscious. And she had been watching the cart and the horses and their moon shadows ever since she recovered from the momentary stunning of her fall. By the intensity of her stare, she was able to discern the form of the tall half-breed – dark upon dark. There had not been even a fractional movement since he collapsed against the cart amid a fusillade of blasting shots. And if Edge was dead . . . Vivid memories crowded into her pain-wracked mind. Of her naked body suffering the worst punishment she could conceive beneath the lusting, thrusting want of a man.

The remembered agony found vocal outlet in a shrill scream. And, as she powered upright and whirled to race up the slope, it was still the memory of the past and not the pain of the present that continued to wrench screams from her.

'She is alive!' the unnamed Mexican yelled. 'I go for her.'

'Do so!' Pedro agreed.

Edge let out his pent-up breath in a silent sigh. And the obscenity he formed to direct at the woman remained in his throat. Just the one man burst out of the house and leapt over the curled form of Manuel: his mind too full with thoughts of Emma to consider that death might still lurk behind the wrecked cart.

Death, in the form of the bullet in the breech of the tight-held Winchester, extended the Mexican's lease on life. Edge ignored the running man and kept all his attention concentrated through the knot hole, his slitted eye not wavering from the lighted doorway and its flanking windows. Pedro was taking the opportunity to run a second test, with his woman-hungry partner as the unwitting reagent.

The running footfalls were heavy and close by. Then they faded, and the man laughed to counterpoint Emma's screams. There were less hurried sounds of movement inside the house.

Then Pedro and Espada stepped outside, guns still drawn and pointed at the tilted cart with the now-quiet horses hitched to the shaft. But Espada could not resist the temptation to divert his smiling attention up the slope – to where his partner was smoothly closing the gap on the stumbling woman.

Which elected Pedro to be the first to die.

Edge powered erect, his glinting-eyed and tight-lipped face and lean torso springing into sight above the cart. Pedro froze, cursed and fired. But his Colt was still aimed at the cart instead of the man behind it. His bullet richocheted off a wheel hub and burrowed into the ground: but he didn't see this. For the half-breed had matched the Mexican's speed in squeezing the trigger. And the Winchester's bullet took Pedro in the heart.

Pedro dropped his gun and staggered backwards. Edge swung the rifle a fraction of an inch and the level of the muzzle neither rose nor fell as he pumped the action. Pedro's heels slammed into the helplessly bound Manuel and the big gunman fell hard and fast. Espada, his stubbled and filthy face contorted into a mask of horror, dropped into a crouch as he tried to take aim. But the Winchester had exploded and the bullet smashed into the centre of his face before the Mexican could put pressure on his trigger.

Espada turned as he collapsed, his gun flying from a loosened grip. An arc of spraying blood from the hole in his top lip hit the ground to measure the extent of the turn. Manuel moaned his terror and tried to struggle out from beneath the second falling man. He didn't make it.

Edge whirled and pumped the Winchester again. His eyes, like slivers of blue ice, raked up the slope. Emma Diamond was still running. But her pursuer had given up the chase. The Mexican had swung into a tight turn and was sprinting across the slope – aiming for the isolated cover of the horse with the broken back. Edge fired and saw blood stream from the man's shoulder. He kept on running. The next bullet drilled into the Mexican's thigh. He tumbled with a scream of alarm rather than pain. Then he hit the ground and bounced into a roll. Edge pumped three more bullets into the man. The final shot ended the scream. The figure smacked into the base of a cactus, folded double, and became inert.

But the half-breed continued to keep the unmoving form covered: his own body as rigid as the Winchester jutting from his shoulder.

'That's enough!' Emma cried, her voice on the brink of hysteria. 'No more, please!'

Edge looked higher up the slope, and saw the woman had reached the crest before she ended the run. Now she was staring downwards, her hands raised with the palms pressed against her ears.

'Manuel!' the woman inside the house cried desperately. 'Manuel!'

'It is all right, my dear,' her husband told her in his native language, ceasing to struggle beneath the weight of the two blood-spilling bodies. 'Our troubles are over.'

Edge canted the rifle to his shoulder and allowed the tenseness to drain out of his stance as Emma lowered her hands and started down the hill. 'Hope you're wrong, feller,' he muttered in English, and moved around the bullet-splintered cart to go towards the house.

The time and work worn face of the aged Mexican expressed heart-felt gratitude as Edge set aside the rifle and stooped to drag off the bodies of Pedro and Espada.

'Bandits, *señor*,' he explained. 'They come here and demand food and a place to sleep. Maria, my wife, she is crippled and has not left her bed for seven years, *señor*. I am old. These men, they think nothing of such things. They were evil and you need have no regret that you killed them, *señor*.'

'Guess I'll learn to live with it,' Edge said sourly as he used the razor to cut away Manuel's bonds.

Manuel had a puffed right eye and a bad bruise on his jaw, showing that his bad treatment from the bandits had started before Edge and Emma had approached his farm. When he tried to rise, he grimaced, groaned and fell again. He forced a brave grin on to his slack mouth. His gums were naked.

'It is difficult when an old man is thrown about and sat on, *señor*.'

Edge became tacitly solicitous and his movements were carefully gentle as he helped the old man to rise to his feet.

'It's because you want something from him,' Emma said coldly as she neared the house, and pointedly avoided looking at the slumped bodies of Pedro and Espada.

Edge ignored her as he draped Manuel's left arm around his own shoulder and half-carried the old man into the house.

'The same as with Tom,' the woman continued as she followed. 'I thought you were being kind to him because he was so badly hurt. But you never do anything without an ulterior motive, do you? You wouldn't give that man the time of day without expecting payment of some kind. Tom gave you information. What do you want here, Mr Edge?'

The house had just the one room. To the left was the sleeping area dominated by a double bed. A thin, grey-haired, wrinkled woman of about sixty lay flat on her back beneath a filthy blanket. On the other side of the room was a cold stove, a table and two chairs. Apart from three wooden crates used to store cooking and eating utensils and a few meagre food supplies, this was the full extent of the furnishings. The light came from an ancient lamp standing on the table, amid the scattered remains of an untidily eaten meal.

'I do not blame your man for this, *señorita*,' Manuel said, trying to placate the coldly angry Emma. 'I do not blame him for what happened when the bandits tried to barter with my life. A man must do – '

'Forget it, feller,' Edge growled as he lowered Manuel on to one of the chairs at the table. 'The lady talks a lot is all.'

On the bed, Maria was staring up at the ceiling. She seemed incapable of moving any muscles except those of her neck. As Edge helped her husband over the threshold, she had craned her head around. Her wrinkled features had expressed pained gratitude that Manuel was alive.

Edge went back to the doorway and Emma stepped aside. The tears of terror, which had coursed through the grime of travel, formed an outline around the base of the bruise which the half-breed's blow had raised on her right cheek. The ebbing fear flooded back across her face as she saw the depth of the cold anger in the hooded eyes. But his hands remained loose and low at his sides.

'I told you to stay up on the hill, ma'am.'

He went out through the doorway she had cleared, retrieved his Winchester and re-entered the house. He started to reload the rifle.

'They were going to kill you!' she defended.

Edge nodded. 'Figured that out for myself. And when my life's on the line, I like to pick my own time for taking the fellers I'm up against.'

'Please do not quarrel,' Manuel put in to finish the period of silence that followed the half-breed's soft-spoken protest. 'It does not matter what has happened. Only that it has happened for the best.'

'We do not have much, *señor*,' the bed-ridden old woman said dully, continuing to gaze at the ceiling. 'But what we have is yours.'

'She says we can have anything they've got,' Edge translated for Emma.

'All I want is for this nightmare to end,' Emma replied flatly, sagging against the doorframe.

Manuel was able to get to his feet unaided now, and the pain this caused took second place on his features to concern for the American woman.

'You must rest, *señorita*,' he insisted as he hobbled towards her. 'You will take my place in the bed. Your man and I will rest on the – '

'He is not my man,' Emma said emphatically. But her voice was the only sign of strength. She was on the point of collapse as she allowed the Mexican to take her hand and lead her to the bed.

'I am sorry, *señorita*,' Manuel soothed, gently turning her around and easing her out full-length alongside his helpless wife. 'I do not wish to offend you.'

Weariness and shock made Emma immune to the squalor of her surroundings. She became as unmoving as the paralysed old woman, and fixed her gaze on the same restricted area of ceiling.

99

'It is not you who do that, *señor*,' she replied to the Mexican. Then she sighed and closed her eyes.

'Do you wish food before you rest?' Manuel asked Edge. 'It will be no trouble to relight the stove.'

The half-breed had rolled a cigarette and now he struck a match. 'Obliged for the offer, feller,' he replied on a cloud of smoke. 'But I'll eat as I go.'

'You're leaving?' Emma exclaimed, raising her head off the evil-smelling pillow. Her suddenly wide eyes were fearful.

'You hired me to do a job, ma'am. And for what you're paying, I don't figure to go to sleep on it.' He peered out through the doorway. 'Not when I'm this close to finishing it, leastways.'

He stepped across the threshold and heard Emma's feet smack against the dirt floor inside the house. He ambled over to the cart, unhitched the two tethered horses and yelled as he slapped them on the rumps. With the smell of burnt powder and drying blood in their nostrils, the animals lunged into an eager gallop up the slope. Edge was halfway to where his gelding stood in the lemon grove when Emma became silhouetted in the lighted doorway of the squalid little house.

'So I can't follow you!' she accused, leaning heavily against the doorframe.

'Right, ma'am,' he confirmed.

'How do I know you'll come back here if you get the money?' Her voice grew shrill, with frustration or perhaps the nearness of hysteria again.

Edge shook his head. 'When.'

'What?'

He grabbed the reins of the gelding and led the animal out from under the trees.

'*When* I get the money, ma'am,' he corrected as he swung up into the saddle. 'It's a matter of a word. You have to accept mine.'

A look of desperation entered her eyes: as they darted from the mounted Edge, to the retreating horses, to the crumpled corpses of Pedro and Espada and then over her shoulder at the Mexican couple. Finally, she returned her gaze to the half-breed. Manuel came up behind her and cupped her elbow in his palm as the rigidity of fear and anger left her.

'All right, Mr Edge,' she said hoarsely. 'Perhaps it's for the best. I might endanger you again. Barney Castle, Tom, these three men . . . so many have died.'

'You forgot the priest, ma'am,' the half-breed muttered.

She nodded. 'Yes, Father Donovan.'

'Makes six, not five,' Edge said as he heeled his horse into an easy walk, angling him towards the base of the slope.

'I haven't kept a tally,' Emma called after him. 'Do I have to apologise for that?'

'No,' he told her over his shoulder. 'Just proves you have to trust me, I guess.'

'I realise I have no alternative,' Emma said stiffly as Manuel urged her back into the house.

Edge's thin lips curled back to show a frigid grin. 'You sure can't count on dead men,' he growled softly.

Chapter Nine

EDGE ate jerked beef and cold beans from the can on the ride back to El Paso. Crossing the Rio Grande, the trail-weary gelding stumbled and pitched him into the night cold waters of the river. The ducking did something to dispel his own tiredness. The thought of the money he was close to earning did a great deal more to hold the threat of exhaustion at bay. Then, as the west Texas town of El Paso came into sight, the white of its adobe buildings showing clearly in the moonlight, the half-breed's strong sense of self-preservation made him as alert as if he had just been roused from a solid night's sleep. Conrad Andrews and the men with whom he rode had come by the money easily. They would not surrender it so.

A few lamps burned in the town, spilling the occasional shaft of yellow out into the pre-dawn darkness. But all of them were turned down to a low wick and the men who were watching Edge were not visible. A baby cried and a dog barked. Several people snored. A woman, or perhaps a child, moaned in a troubled sleep. The hooves of the gelding beat slow time on the hard-packed dirt of the streets, then halted on Division, outside the Holden House. The watchers made no move against Edge. As the best El Paso had to offer, it wasn't much of a place. A combination of frame and adobe, it had a raised stoop, with a railed balcony above, which was shared by all the second floor front rooms. The only light showed through the frosted-glass panels of the closed doors giving on to the lobby. It wasn't much brighter when Edge opened one of the doors and stepped across the threshold. The source was a lamp standing on the desk at one side of the lobby, opposite the stairway.

The night clerk had been using the lamp to read a dime novel. But the excitement of the reading had been too much or not enough. He was perched on a stool and slumped forward across the desk. His breathing was a true clue to the deepness of his sleep. He did not stir as the tall half-breed crossed the lobby.

Edge wrinkled his nose to the smell of cheap whiskey before he saw the bottle – three-quarters empty and still uncapped – standing behind the lamp. He halted in front of the desk and eased the Winchester away from his shoulder. He allowed the barrel free fall until it was six inches above the head of the sleeping clerk. Then he flicked his wrist to add power to the blow. A thick padding of black hair muted the sound of barrel against head. The clerk slipped from natural sleep into unconsciousness with nothing more than an irritated grunt.

'You'd have had a headache anyway, feller,' Edge muttered as he leaned over the desk and drew the register from a shelf beneath.

He flipped the book open to a marked page and ran a grimed finger down the list of recent entries. The Jap had signed in with the characters of his native language. He had the neatest hand. Conrad Andrews' signature and those of George and Harry Hare were just decipherable. There were two crosses which presumably were the marks of Kenyon Lamb and Ira Walker.

Each man had been allotted a separate room on the second floor of the hotel. Four other rooms in the Holden House were occupied and five were vacant.

Edge closed the book and returned it to the shelf. It took him a full minute to locate the pass key, which was in the hip pocket of the unconscious clerk. Then he crossed the lobby and moved quietly up the stairway. At the top, he paused, allowing his eyes to adjust to the darkened landing. The door to room seven was nearest the top of the stairs. One of the men who was unable to write had drawn this room. Edge keyed open the door, cracked it, slid inside, and closed it. A man was breathing as deeply and regularly as the clerk down in the lobby.

The half-breed padded silently over the uncarpeted floor-boards. The rhythm of the sleeping man's breathing did not alter. Just his head was visible, above the dark blanket and against the white linen of the pillow. His teeth were showing in a quiet grin as he dreamed of something pleasant.

After Edge stooped, laid the Winchester on the floor and drew the razor, he looked more closely at the face on the pillow. It appeared almost fleshless, the skin hanging loosely between the high points of the bones.

'You got to be Ira Walker,' the half-breed whispered, clamping a hand over the man's mouth and resting the razor against the throat.

The gaunt man awoke with a start, his eyes snapping wide and filled with terror. Edge lowered himself on to the side of the bed and pressed a little harder with the razor.

'Going to let you talk, feller. But if you don't do it right, you won't have the time to make any more mistakes. You got the idea?'

He raised his hand away from the man's mouth. The tongue came out as if to lick away the taste of Edge's touch from his lips. 'That a knife you got against my throat?' he whispered.

'Close enough,' Edge answered. 'You Walker?'

'Yeah. What is this?'

'What's known as a rude awakening, feller. But we can keep it polite if you forget about asking questions and just answer them. Your share in the room here?'

'Share?'

Edge clamped his hand back over Walker's mouth, tilted the razor and dragged it down the man's throat a half inch. A sliver of skin was flaked off and Walker struggled.

'Answers, remember?' Edge said, and raised his hand from the mouth. Walker became still. 'And remember something else, feller. You're just one of a pack. So I can afford to make a lot of cuts.'

'Con and the rest of the boys – '

'Are sleeping,' the half-breed interrupted. 'You want to wake them? Won't cost you anything but your life.'

The man's Adam's apple bobbed against the pressure of the razor's blade. Not enough to draw blood.. But Walker felt the keenness of the honed metal.

'I guess you gotta be talkin' about my share of what we took outta the grave, huh?'

Edge showed an icy grin. 'Now you're getting the idea.'

'Saddlebags in the corner,' Walker rasped. 'I told Con we should've just killed Tom Diamond 'stead of foolin' around with that slow death crap. He pointed the finger to here, I bet.'

Edge shook his head. 'You can't afford to bet, feller. You're broke.'

'Tom's sister Emma hired you, I guess.'

'A mind like you got, you should have learned to write, feller. What's your share?'

He grimaced. 'Twenty grand, the same as Con's. On account I helped Tom bust out of the pen and told Con old man Diamond could get took for a bundle. Then it was my idea to take it outta the grave after the old man kicked the bucket. Others got fifteen thou apiece after Tom was wasted for tryin' to get greedy. Wanted half.'

'Much spent?'

Another grimace. 'Drop in the friggin' ocean when you're talkin' about that kinda bundle. Livin's cheap in El Paso.'

'Same as dying anyplace,' the half-breed replied.

'Mister, I'm doin' like you asked and you – '

Edge clamped Walker's mouth as the man's voice started to rise with his fear. 'Sure, feller, you did everything was asked of you,' he said in a soothing tone. 'You can go back to sleep now.'

Fear became confusion in the sunken eyes. Then, as Edge started to rise from the bed, Ira Walker betrayed a flicker of defiant hope. As the pressure of the razor was removed from his throat and the hand lifted away from his mouth, he sucked in a gulp of air. His lips parted to vent a yell.

But the half-breed's apparent carelessness was a false front: designed to lull Walker into a sense of security and break the man's concentration. Thus, as Walker thought he saw an opportunity to turn the tables, Edge swung into a lightning attack. The hand which had clamped the mouth dropped to cup the crown of Walker's head. That gripping the razor clenched into an even tighter fist. And the bunched knuckles slammed with vicious power into the point of Walker's jaw.

The man could not move his head a fraction of an inch. His open mouth slammed closed. The teeth crashed together and there was a muted but horrific cracking of shattered enamel. Walker was unconscious within an instant, but he threatened to wake his partners with choking sounds as pieces of his teeth rained against the back of his throat and were involuntarily rejected.

Edge bunched a fistful of the man's hair and jerked him upright, then pushed his head down towards his chest. The broken jaw fell open and fragments of teeth spilled out on a stream of blood from burst gums.

Edge looked ruefully at his knuckles after he had sheathed the razor. 'Guess that makes my bark worse than your bite, feller,' he muttered.

He went to the corner where Walker's gear was untidily stowed and returned to the bed with the saddlebags. He upended them to spill out the contents. Amongst the lesser necessities of life there were nineteen bundles of bills, each held together by a paper band. All the bills were tens. Edge decided he had neither the time to count the money, nor any reason to doubt that there was an even thousand in each bundle.

Walker's clothes were strewn beneath the bed and the hip pocket of the pants produced a further seven hundred dollars. Loose change rattled in another pocket, but he ignored the coins and jerked the blanket off the unconscious man. Walker slept in longjohns which he had neglected to button after completing his final chore before going to bed.

Edge went to the door, opened it and looked along the landing. It was as dark and as quiet as before. Back at the bed, he pushed the money inside his shirt. Then he wrapped Walker in the blanket and slung the limp form over his shoulder. He canted the Winchester to his other shoulder and went out of the room and down the stairs. Walker did not have enough flesh on his bones to be heavy and just a single stair tread creaked under the weight of two men. The clerk was still slumped across the desk.

The half-breed went to the desk, rested the rifle for a moment, and took a deep swig from the uncapped whiskey bottle. The almost raw liquor burned all the way down and started a fire in his belly. But its effect had dissipated by the time he had draped Walker over the gelding, mounted and rode the horse at a gentle walk across the quiet town to the law office. A dim light burned behind the lettered windows and he could see a man sitting behind the desk. The same tall, broadly built man who had visited the back room at the Bella Cantina.

The sheriff was not asleep. As the gelding was halted, to curtail the only sound in this part of El Paso, the man rose from the chair and moved around the desk to approach the door. After he had swung it open and stepped on to the threshold, he dropped his right hand to cup the butt of the holstered gun at his thigh.

'You look like you were expecting me, feller,' Edge said, hooking the fingers of each hand together and resting them on the curved back of the blanket-wrapped Walker.

'Run a tight town by stoppin' trouble before it has a chance to start,' the sheriff replied in his lazy drawl. 'Have to keep watchin' and listenin' to do that, Mr Edge. My deputies had their eye on you ever since you rode back into El Paso. He dead?'

'Banged his jaw into my fist is all,' Edge supplied.

The sheriff nodded. 'Figured somethin' like that. Or you wouldn't have come ridin' up here like you did – after what I told you at the cantina. What's on your mind?'

'Same thing that's on yours, I guess. El Paso has got some dirt in it. Like to clear it out. Won't be no trouble, feller.'

The lawman smiled. 'You mean for me?'

Edge did not respond to the smile. 'You made your position pretty clear and I got the message.'

A nod that finished the smile. 'I've got your position clear, Edge. Got to thinkin' about you after you left and I ran through my wanted bills. Found an old flyer put out by the law in a Kansas town. You don't look much like the picture of Josiah C. Hedges. But you look enough like him.'

Edge pursed his lips. 'One flyer for one killing is enough. And it could be somebody'll have to die for me to get what I want.'

'Maybe more than one,' the lawman drawled. 'You think his buddies will care that much about him?' He pointed at the slumped form of Ira Walker.

'If you tell them I aim to get them all. And you also tell them I'll be two hours fast riding across the Rio Grande. Due south.'

'How would I know that?'

'Because I told you.'

'To send them into a trap?'

'My gamble, feller. All you got to lose are five big-spending tourists.'

The sheriff nodded. 'I'll tell them. When?'

'When they wake up.'

'All right.'

Edge gave a curt nod of farewell and turned the gelding.

'One thing, Edge,' the sheriff called, his tone abruptly hard.

The half-breed looked back over his shoulder at the tall man silhouetted against the light from the law office doorway.

'What'll I tell the room clerk about the lump on his head?'

'You have to expect things like that in those big old buildings,' Edge replied lightly, and showed his own brand of quiet grin.

'What things?' the sheriff asked.

'The kind that go bump in the night.'

Chapter Ten

THE sun was up and harshly hot when Edge rode down the slope towards the squalid little farm house on the plain to the east of the Sierra Madre. The smell of breakfast – and the two dead horses – was tainting the citrus-strong air. But there was no longer smoke rising from the chimney. Manuel limped into the open doorway as Edge swung out of the saddle and led the gelding towards the stable. Emma Diamond, her right cheek black with the bruise, gazed miserably out of one of the glassless windows.

'Now I understand what you meant last night, *señor*,' the Mexican said wearily.

Edge took the gelding into the dilapidated stable without responding. A thin burro with sores on his belly and hind-quarters eyed the newcomers with distaste and anger. He bared his teeth in a snarl and pulled at his restraining rope. But then he submitted to the intrusion and concentrated upon swatting at the flies with his tail.

'I know just how you feel, mule!' Ira Walker growled.

Edge continued to ignore his prisoner as he lifted him off the gelding and dropped him dispassionately to the straw-spread floor. He had failed to respond to every complaint Walker had made since the crossing of the Rio Grande had revived the man. The blanket had been tied around him with a lariat rope since he came out of unconsciousness, and his discomfort had increased by degrees as the heat of the rising sun grew harsher.

When the gelding was unsaddled, Edge put down feed for him, and transferred the water pail from the burro's stall to where the horse was tethered. Only then did he use the razor to cut through the ropes binding Walker.

'Button it up,' the half-breed ordered.

'Ain't no point in openin' it where you're concerned, mister,' the gaunt-faced man snarled. 'You ain't no talker.'

'I'm talking now. And not about your mouth.' He jabbed the muzzle of the Winchester into Walker's exposed crotch. 'There are ladies around.'

The man grunted with the pain of the blow, then fastened his longjohns. Edge moved behind him and this time jabbed the rifle at the small of Walker's back. Walker staggered out into the bright sunlight, still weak from unconsciousness and more than three hours riding in such an unnatural position.

'I said I understand what you meant last night, señor,' Manuel insisted. 'When you say you hope trouble is not over for Maria and me. You bring it here again.'

Walker saw Emma at the window and recognised her. He halted and looked back at Edge. His bloodied and broken jaw gaped in a permanent expression of pained surprise. But his dark, deep-set eyes were able to show independence. They expressed fear now.

'Look, the Jap always likes his own way,' he pleaded. Despite the broken bone in his lower face, he was able to pronounce words distinctly.

'Just move on over to the window, feller,' Edge urged, and Walker complied before the rifle muzzle punished him once more.

'This is one of them?' Emma asked dully.

Manuel remained where he was in the doorway, miserably

resigned to whatever was going to happen. Behind Emma, the bed-ridden old Mexican woman raised her head for a fleeting glance towards the window, then returned to her enforced contemplation of the ceiling.

'Ira Walker,' Edge answered evenly. 'Your brother's buddy. Helped Tom to break out of prison. Had charge of what happened out at the river because it was his idea. Gave the Jap the go-ahead to – '

'You seem to have punished him,' Emma interrupted, showing pity as she grimaced at the sight of Walker's broken jaw and the shattered teeth in the blood-caked gums.

'That was to keep him quiet, ma'am,' the half-breed answered, and ambled towards the door. Manuel stood aside to allow Edge to step inside the house. 'Punishment's up to you.'

Nobody had eaten the breakfast that had been prepared. The bacon and beans were a congealed mess on the three plates on the table.

'I leave punishment to the Lord,' Emma replied.

Except for the old Mexican, Walker was alone outside the house. He looked hurriedly about him, but the vista of dry and near barren terrain, in combination with his injury and lack of protective clothing, merely added despair to desperation. He returned his gaze to Emma across the window sill.

'I did you a favour, ma'am,' he implored. 'I'd said no, the Jap would just've gone ahead anyway. And he'd have been feelin' real mean as well as horny . . . beg your pardon, Miss Diamond, ma'am.'

There was some ready-cut bread on the table and Edge chewed on a hunk, passing up the rancid butter. The coffee pot was warm to the touch and he poured some of the tepid liquid into a mug and drank.

'They killed your brother because he wanted too much of the take,' Edge supplied.

'But I didn't wanna make him suffer the way he did, Miss Diamond!' Walker defended. 'That was the others.'

'Where are the others?' Emma asked, and half turned to look at Edge.

He unfastened his shirt and started to unload the bundles of

111

money. Manuel stared in awe at the mounting pile of bills.

'Back in El Paso,' Walker supplied. 'He just brung me.'

'On their way here, I figure,' Edge countered. He placed the loose seven hundred on top of the heap of money and continued with his meal. 'Walker's share, less the three hundred he's spent.'

Manuel abruptly lost interest in the money on the table. 'More bad men are coming here to my place, *señor*? So much trouble you bring. And my wife, she is very sick. Both of us are very old.' He held his shaking hands out in front of him. 'To bury the three bandits used all my strength, *señor*.'

Emma gave an emphatic nod. 'Manuel is right, Mr Edge! He and his wife do not deserve any more trouble. We will go to El Paso and take our chances with that coward of a sheriff.'

'What about me, Miss Diamond?' Walker demanded.

Emma considered herself fully in command of the situation. 'You will return with us and be handed over to the custody of the law.' She returned her hard-eyed attention to Edge. 'And if we get no satisfaction at local level, we will approach the state authorities.'

'No way, ma'am,' the half-breed told her evenly, and then stifled a yawn. 'You hired me to do a job and I aim to finish it.'

'Yes, I hired you!' Emma snapped. 'Which means I can also fire you! We can discuss severance pay, which you may take from the portion of the money you have recovered.'

In her own language, Maria asked her husband what was happening. The old man shuffled across to sit on the side of the bed and began to talk to her in low tones.

'Bad time, ma'am,' Edge said, and didn't try to stop the yawn.

'You have brought it upon yourself!' Emma retorted stiffly.

The half-breed used a finger to print calculations in the dust of the table top. 'I'll take ten per cent, as agreed. That comes out at nineteen-seventy dollars. Leaves you plenty to buy the old feller's burro and maybe a gun if he's got one around the place.'

'Come on, ma'am!' Walker urged. 'If that's the way he wants it.'

'I have only very old gun, *señor*,' Manuel said miserably. 'Must keep burro.'

'I have no use for a gun,' Emma snapped, directing her ire at Edge as he began to take the specified amount from the pile of bills.

'But her mouth's in better shape than your's, Walker,' the half-breed drawled. 'She likes to talk. You figure she'll be able to talk faster than the Jap can jump?'

The confidence drained out of Emma's face and body. There was still a lot of anger in her, but it was trapped by speechless frustration.

'I'll protect you, Miss Diamond, ma'am!' Walker urged. 'If they're comin' like he reckons they are, I'll tell them to leave you alone.' As the woman swung around to give him a helpless look, he realised the foolishness of the claim. 'Or we could take a roundabout way back, Miss Diamond, ma'am. Swing wide so that we miss them?'

Emma shook her head. 'It's no good, Mr Walker. Things are too well advanced the way Mr Edge has planned them.'

The former despair crowded into the gaunt man's eyes.

'The lady's always changing her mind, feller,' Edge said, dropping the handful of bills back on the pile.

'You're . . . ' Emma started.

'Insufferable, I know,' Edge said, rising from the table and finishing the last of the coffee from the mug. 'But seeing as how you've decided to suffer me a little longer, what about giving me a hand. Be a switch from all the mouth I've been getting from you.'

'I've got no alternative but to help you, I suppose,' Emma groaned. Then her voice became a snarl. 'But you're an easy man to hate, Mr Edge!'

The half-breed grinned. 'You should keep your Pa's money, ma'am.'

'I would never dream of doing that!'

Edge shrugged. 'Then I guess you got to keep on living from hand to mouth.'

8

Chapter Eleven

CONRAD ANDREWS and his four men crested the rise above the farm abreast and reined their mounts to a halt. Hands which had rested on holstered revolvers swung away to reach for more fire power. The Hare brothers, Kenyon Lamb and the Jap slid repeater rifles from their saddle boots and pumped the actions. Andrews moved the double-barrelled shotgun from across his back to point down the slope. His thumb cocked both hammers.

It was almost noon, for they had slept late. But they had ridden hard after getting the message from the lawman. It showed in the sweaty weariness of riders and mounts alike.

'You reckon this is the place, Con?' Lamb asked after all five men had peered suspiciously at the farm house and stable for long moments.

'Looks like there ain't no one there,' George Hare said in his low-pitched, Southern drawl.

'Things ain't always like they look, you know what I mean?' Andrews growled, wiping away the sweat from his forehead with a meaty forearm.

'One man,' the Jap reminded, then smiled evilly at a memory. 'Maybe with little missy.'

Harry Hare was six inches taller than his brother's five-and-a-half feet. He was seven years older and far less impetuous. 'If there is just the one critter, Con, he ain't no crazy man. He ain't just sittin' down there and waitin' for us to come a runnin'.'

Andrews spat to the side without taking his eyes away from the scene spread out in front of him. 'Maybe that's just what the guy is doin', Harry,' he countered evenly. 'Out on this slope, he would pick us off like bugs on a floor with no cracks in it – you know what I mean?'

'Horse looks fresh dead,' Lamb put in, nodding towards the black gelding with the broken back.

'He don't smell it,' George Hare replied with a grimace.

'It's the heat,' Harry Hare explained.

'I say spread out on all sides and rush him, the bastard!' the Jap said.

'Wait 'til night and go in slow, I reckon,' Lamb suggested.

'Still figure we should've called his bluff and stuck in Paso,' George growled.

'I got too much in the pot to play a bluff game – you know what I mean?' Andrews rasped, patting a bulging saddlebag as he fixed the younger Hare with a cold stare.

'The kid is just talkin' to pass the time,' Harry said hurriedly, sweeping a glare of his own at his brother. 'He's like the rest of us. Don't want always to be lookin' over his shoulder for the guy the dame hired.'

'That right, kid?' Andrews demanded.

George nodded. 'Sure, Con. But now we're here, we gotta do somethin' 'cept look.' He gazed scornfully down the slope. 'If this is the place, even.'

'If it is and he's down there, he's sure enough seen us,' Lamb said in a complaining tone.

'Look!' the Jap snarled.

'The well!' Ira Walker yelled as he plunged out of the open doorway. And screamed as his broken jaw protested the need to gape so wide for the panicked shout. 'In the Goddamn well, Con!'

115

The men on the hill crest grunted their surprise at the sudden appearance of Walker. And clearly heard the shrieked warning from his blood-crusted mouth. Then, as he turned and raced across the front of the house, they saw that his hands were tied behind his back.

A moment later, as Walker – still clad only in his underwear – scuttled clear of the doorway, a gun exploded. Its report resounded like a clap of summer thunder in the confines of the well. It was a scatter-gun and the shot belched from its broad muzzle ripped adobe from the doorframe. Walker screamed again, but kept on running, aiming for the cover of the lemon grove.

'Blast it!' Andrews snarled, and thudded in his heels to spur his mount into a gallop down the slope.

The other four responded immediately, plunging on to the slope only feet behind the big man. Controlling their horses with spurred heels and knees, they threw rifle stocks to their shoulders and rained lead towards the well. The bullets cracked out of the cloud of moving dust made by the horses – and smacked into the well wall. The range narrowed and the constant barrage turned adobe into powder as countless holes were drilled into the target. There was not a chance in a million that a second shot could be exploded from the shattered cover.

Then, as the galloping horses carried the sweating riders on to the level ground fronting the house, Andrews spurred his horse into greater speed while the other men ceased fire to rein in their mounts. A grin of triumph splitting his bearded face, the big man squeezed one of the triggers of the shotgun. The range was but a few feet now, and the charge blasted against the wall and caved in a length of the bullet-pocked adobe. Still Andrews did not slow his mount. He merely canted the smoking muzzle of the shotgun towards the ground – rode close to the wall, and emptied the second barrel into the smoke-and-dust filled mouth of the well.

'We showed him, Ira!' he yelled as he released the shotgun and gathered up the reins to bring his horse to a rearing halt.

'Where is missy?' the Jap shouted, his enormous weight hitting the ground hard as he slid from the saddle.

116

Lamb and the Hare brothers were quick to follow his actions. But, instead of standing and peering around through the settling dust, they ran towards the wreckage of the well wall, and stared down.

'Con!' Walker shrieked, forcing himself up on to his knees from where he had flung himself to the ground in the lemon grove.

- 'Good to see you!' Andrews yelled, kicking free of his stirrups and leaping to the ground in front of the grove. 'We still got us a great team, don't we – you know what I mean?'

'A friggin' wire!' the Jap roared, and pointed.

'You had to get the message sometime,' Edge said as he stepped into the shot-blackened doorway of the house.

'I couldn't do any . . .' Ira Walker pleaded as Andrews' suddenly hate-filled eyes swung back to the kneeling man after his stunned gaze had swept towards the half-breed.

The excuse he had started to make was valid.

Edge had seen the five men as they rode to the hill crest and halted their horses to survey the farm. He was crouched against the rear wall of the one-roomed house, hidden in the deep shade, but able to see broad areas of the slope through the windows and open door.

The trembling Ira Walker had stood against the opposite wall, pressed to the adobe between the door and one of the windows. His eyes had pleaded for mercy, but he had dared not speak after Edge quietly warned him his partners were on the hill. And, although aware that a shot from the levelled Winchester would alert Andrews and the others, he was not prepared to risk his slender chance of life for the benefit of the men on the hill crest. So he stayed sweating and trembling and silent, having to trust the tall, dark-skinned half-breed to keep his word and give him that chance.

'They're anxious enough,' Edge had muttered across the fetid room. 'Go!'

And Walker had sent a final silent plea towards Edge, then swung away from the wall and lunged out of the doorway. An instant after shouting the warning he had been instructed to give, he had purposely tripped the length of twine strung low

117

across the dust from the doorway to a hole in the well wall. The jerk of the twine had pulled the trigger of Manuel's ancient scattergun lodged in the well mouth.

The watching men had been keyed up enough to believe the evidence of their own ears and eyes.

Now, the Jap, Lamb and the Hare brothers looked from the exposed wire towards the tall, lean man in the doorway. And Andrews glared at the trembling Walker.

'Put up your hands, please,' Emma Diamond demanded shrilly as she stepped out of the stable doorway.

The four men in front of the house had booted their rifles before dismounting.

'Fat chance!' Lamb snarled.

He was first to reach for his holstered revolver. But the others were only a split-second behind him.

'Crazy lady;' Edge rasped, and squeezed the Winchester's trigger.

The medium-built Lamb took the .44 calibre bullet in the centre of his heart and died on his feet. He staggered backwards, driven by the impact of the bullet, hit the crumbled adobe of the well wall and tipped over into the hole.

Emma screamed and whirled to run back into the stable.

'Fitting Lamb leads the slaughter,' the half-breed growled as he slammed his back against the inside wall of the house.

Bullets from the guns of the Jap and the two brothers cracked through the doorway where, an instant before, Edge had been standing.

A fourth shot exploded and the enraged Andrews whirled away from the crumpling, bloody-faced Ira Walker. The kneeling man had been executed with a bullet in the centre of his forehead from the avenging handgun of the gang leader towering above him. Then, as the horses bolted from the deafening barrage of gunfire and the acrid stench of burnt powder, Andrews lunged into the grove and swung his shotgun around from his back.

'I didn't want you killed!' Emma screamed as the Jap and the Hare brothers threw themselves down behind the shattered well

118

wall and blasted another fusillade of shots through the house doorway.

Manuel shrieked a Spanish curse.

'No, please!' Emma protested.

A revolver shot cracked from the stable.

'Damn, there's a friggin' army!' George Hare snarled as the bullet skimmed across the top of his head.

Edge stepped into a window as George scampered around the wall. The Winchester thudded a recoil against his shoulder and he saw the younger Hare jerk and become still – blood spurting from a ragged hole in the side of his head. Then he powered down into a crouch as two bullets cracked through the window to dig holes in the rear wall.

'You bastard!' Harry snarled. 'You killed my brother!'

He lunged upright and raced towards the doorway. The Jap covered him, going up on one knee and swinging his gun arm in confined arcs. Alternate bullets whined through the window where Edge had last showed, and splintered wood from the stable door.

The gun of the grief-stricken Harry rattled empty as he followed the last bullet into the house. Edge was squatting against the wall to the left of the doorway. As the hysterical man's leading foot appeared, the half-breed powered erect and swung into a half turn. His right hand streaked away from the nape of his neck and the blade of the razor glinted with the same brand of menace that showed in his narrowed eyes.

Harry's forward momentum, as much as the strength of the attacker's arm, sank the blade into the centre of the belly, just above the belt buckle. But, as one man screamed and the other completed straightening, it was entirely the power of the half-breed that ripped the blade through Harry's flesh, tearing him open from navel to throat.

A welter of half-digested food spilled out and a great torrent of bubbling crimson sprayed in its wake. The mutilated man, silent in the throat now, followed his spillage to the floor.

'Go see George, Harry,' Edge rasped as he wiped both sides of the blade on the dead man's back and returned the razor to its neck pouch. 'Ain't no one can accuse me of splitting Hares.'

Stretched seconds had slid into history without a shot being fired. Edge went down into a crouch and peered out through the doorway. The short, fat Jap was on his feet. The fear in his Oriental eyes as they flicked a gaze between the stable and the house betrayed that the gun in his trembling hand was empty.

'Please give yourself up!' Emma pleaded.

Her voice triggered him into action, sending him into a waddling run towards the lemon grove.

'No more!' Emma shrieked.

A gunshot blasted, but the bullet burrowed into the ground four feet beyond the stable doorway as the woman spoiled Manuel's aim. The Mexican cursed.

Edge swung into the doorway as he drew himself erect. He took aim on the running man. Then saw the shadow of another man – growing away from the end of patch of shade that marked the roofline of the house.

The Jap snatched a look back over his shoulder to see if the plan Andrews had signalled was working. His mouth gaped to shout a warning.

Edge dived out through the doorway, kicking into a mid-air turn. His first shot exploded while he was still clear of the ground. Andrews grunted as it tore into his upper arm. The shotgun was already pointed downwards and the finger curled around both triggers. The shock of the wound jerked a nerve in his finger.

Both barrels of the shotgun belched their lethal charges. The scattering loads blasted a gaping hole in the house roof and tore the body of Harry Hare to pieces.

Edge worked the action of the Winchester as he thudded to the ground on his back.

'You stinkin' – ' Andrews started as he went for his holstered Colt and dropped into a crouch.

Only his head was above the roofline and Edge's shot entered between the anger-flared nostrils and exited at the crown of the skull. Andrews flipped backwards from the crouch, his feet kicking out from under him. His legs plunged into the hole ripped by the shotgun. His torso and head smacked against the roof. He teetered for a moment, then slid downwards. His boots squelched into the pulped and bloody flesh of Hare. For an instant, he seemed to stand there, upright. Then his body crumpled into the shattered remains. The crimson flow from the awesome wounds of the two men merged.

Heavy footfalls thudded against the baking ground of Mexico.

'Let him go!' Emma yelled.

Edge turned and saw that the Jap posed no threat – except to some of the money. The horses were scattered over the hill slope, but they had halted, exhausted by the bolts after the hard ride from El Paso. The closest animal – the one to which the Jap was heading – was Andrews' mount. There was no rifle boot hung from the saddle.

The Winchester thudded to the half-breed's shoulder as he folded up into a sitting position and spun on his rump to aim at the Jap. The rifle exploded as the fleeing man got one foot in the stirrup and heaved himself up to straddle the horse. The bullet took him in the side, high up on the left. It had enough velocity to burrow between two ribs and find the heart. And the impact was powerful enough to hurl the victim through the air in a short arc.

'Didn't get any colder,' Edge muttered wryly as the Jap's body thudded to the ground and he used the rifle as a lever to ease his weary body upright.

'Why?' Emma demanded, stumbling from the stable.

'Figured there was a Nip in the air,' Edge replied through a yawn.

'You beast!' the woman snapped. 'You know what I . . . why did you kill him?'

Edge spat as the woman skidded to a halt in the doorway and stared in near-fainting horror at the body of Conrad Andrews sprawled across the pulped flesh of Harry Hare.

'Twenty thousand reasons, less El Paso cost of living expenses.'

'I try to help, *señor*,' Manuel called from the stable. 'But the *señorita* – she keep spoiling my aim. You help me get Maria's bed back in the house now, *por favor*?'

Emma Diamond chewed on her lower lip and clenched her

fists to fight back the nausea and keep from passing out. The anger and shrillness had gone from her voice.

'They were all murderers and thieves,' she said dully, still gazing at the big man with his brains spilled out of the top of his skull. 'But he was the worst, I suppose. He was the leader. He was totally evil, wasn't he, Mr Edge?'

The half-breed bared his teeth as he glanced at the gang's top man. 'Guess that says it all, ma'am,' he growled. 'Almost time to close the book. Andrews, that was your life.'

Chapter Twelve

IT was seven days later when they returned to the grave of Boyce Diamond and Emma asked Edge to disturb the old man's resting place again.

For the rest of the day and the night that followed the slaughter at the farm of Manuel and Maria, the half-breed had slept in the stable. His final chore before bedding down had been to round-up the scattered horses and collect the money from the saddlebags. When the bills were added to those Edge had taken from Ira Walker, the total came to a little over two thousand short of what the gang had stolen from the grave.

Edge had claimed his money.

And gone to sleep for a solid sixteen hours.

When he was roused by Emma, the dead were buried, the old woman and her bed were back in the cleaned and repaired house, and Manuel was ecstatically grateful to be repaid for his trouble with four horses and all their tack. Emma took the fifth one to replace her dead gelding.

She didn't ask Edge to escort her back to the Big Bend

country of the Rio Grande, but she made no objection when he did. On the long ride – in Mexico for most of the way, until they crossed the river west of Dream Creek – she was distantly polite: speaking only when it was strictly necessary, and doing her share of the chores.

In the town where sheepmen had found the haven they dreamed about and had given it an appropriate name, Emma called a temporary halt to retrieve the suitcase she had left in the care of the Bonnington Hotel. The couple were greeted with surprised, but silent curiosity: and both of them sensed a certain air of relief behind them as they left town, still heading eastwards.

Sheriff Schabar trailed them, matching their easy pace and holding off a long way back. And he was out of sight over the rise above the river bank when Emma asked Edge to open the grave while she climbed up to one of the caves, dragging her suitcase with her.

It was mid-afternoon and the sun was as blistering hot as it had ever been on either side of the river. Edge sweated as he worked with the shovel, which Emma had carried on her horse all the way from the Mexican farm. The loose, dusty soil was easy to move and it took only a few minutes to get down to the pine lid of the casket.

The big-boned lawman came into sight then, and rode his horse at the same easy pace down the slope to the river bank. His expression was as impassive as that of the half-breed as he reined his mount to a halt.

'Where's Miss Diamond?' Schabar asked.

The casket lid was already loose from where it had been prised open by the grave-robbers. A single wrench with the shovel lifted it again.

'Around someplace,' Edge answered as he heaved himself up out of the hole and looked down at the putrefying corpse of Boyce Diamond.

Schabar's eyes raked the empty land along the river's north bank. Then he drew his Remington. Fast and smooth. The sweat stains on his shirt at the armpits expanded as the half-breed watched.

124

'She got hardly anything right,' Edge rasped, canting the shovel to his shoulder as if it were his Winchester. 'She figured you were trailing us to protect her.'

'If you killed her, it saves me the trouble, mister,' Schabar said, not taking his small eyes off Edge's nonchalantly-set features. 'That saddlebag got the money in it?'

Before going up to the cave, Emma had unhooked a single bag from her saddlehorn and dropped it near the graveside.

'You want to take a look, feller?'

The lawman responded with a curt nod. 'You open it!'

Edge squatted, rested the shovel and worked on the bag buckle with loose, easy-moving fingers.

'Only you, me and the woman know about what that crazy old guy wanted done with his loot,' Schabar said, a hint of excitement entering his tone. 'Guess you must have figured that out for yourself – and reckoned why shouldn't you keep the whole bundle?'

'So why did I open the grave, feller?' Edge asked evenly as the strap was unfastened and he rose to his full height. 'For once, the lady listened to me.' He upended the bag over the grave. 'He ain't quite it yet: but, ashes to dust. Close enough.'

Schabar shifted his gaze now, to stare in awe at the blackened remains of almost ninety thousand dollars pouring from the bag into the open casket.

Then the anger of frustration gripped him and he vented a bellow as he swung his eyes to match the direction of the gun barrel.

'Sheriff!' Emma Diamond shrieked, an instant before Schabar's white-knuckled finger triggered the Remington.

The glance up the slope to the cave mouth might have been nothing more than that. But the sight on the hill forced the lawman into a fatal double-take. Edge's Colt slid from the holster ready-cocked and the bullet it exploded crashed into the flesh of Schabar's throat. The big man was hurled off his horse and slammed to the ground. The baked earth sucked thirstily at the gushing arterial blood, battling with a swarm of flies for the larger share.

Schabar had died instantaneously. He carried into death a

startling image of Emma Diamond, totally naked: displaying every curve and indentation of her slender body – the brilliant sunlight giving her flesh an almost translucent quality against the dark shade of the cave mouth behind her.

She stood there for a moment, as Edge holstered his smoking revolver and looked up at her from beside the slumped body of Schabar. Then she shrieked, whirled and lunged back into the cave.

'Don't you dare come up here, Mr Edge!' she screamed, her voice echoing between the walls of the cave.

Edge picked up the shovel, reached down into the grave and nudged the lid back on the casket to hide the body and the black ashes. He showed a wry grin as he began to heap the earth back into the hole.

'Fitting she sounds distracted, ain't it, feller,' he muttered to the fresher corpse above ground.

He had finished the chore when she called his name to draw his attention back to the cave in the hillside. Her riding clothes had been discarded and her nakedness of a few minutes ago was entirely covered. He looked at her in silence for long moments, recalling so many of the things she had said and done which had seemed strange at the time.

'It was not a suitable attire for the work I had to do, Mr Edge.'

'Guess not, Sister,' he answered.

Emma Diamond was a Sister of Mercy, her hair drawn severely back and trapped beneath a starched white whimple that contrasted starkly with the jet black of her cowl and the mantle that swept to the ground.

She smiled wanly as she started down the slope. 'You see it all now, Mr Edge?' she suggested softly.

'Not as much as I saw awhile back,' the half-breed replied with a sigh. 'But it sure explains why I didn't get nun of it.'

THE END

126

NEL BESTSELLERS

Crime

T017 095	LORD PETER VIEWS THE BODY	Dorothy L. Sayers	40p
T026 663	THE DOCUMENTS IN THE CASE	Dorothy L. Sayers	50p
T027 821	GAUDY NIGHT	Dorothy L. Sayers	75p
T023 923	STRONG POISON	Dorothy L. Sayers	45p
T026 671	FIVE RED HERRINGS	Dorothy L. Sayers	50p
T025 462	MURDER MUST ADVERTISE	Dorothy L. Sayers	50p

Fiction

T029 522	HATTER'S CASTLE	A. J. Cronin	£1.00
T027 228	THE SPANISH GARDNER	A. J. Cronin	45p
T013 936	THE JUDAS TREE	A. J. Cronin	50p
T015 386	THE NORTHERN LIGHT	A. J. Cronin	50p
T026 213	THE CITADEL	A. J. Cronin	80p
T027 112	BEYOND THIS PLACE	A. J. Cronin	60p
T016 609	KEYS OF THE KINGDOM	A. J. Cronin	60p
T029 158	THE STARS LOOK DOWN	A. J. Cronin	£1.00
T022 021	THREE LOVES	A. J. Cronin	90p
T003 922	IN THE COMPANY OF EAGLES	Ernest K. Gann	30p
T022 536	THE HARRAD EXPERIMENTS	Robert H. Rimmer	50p
T022 994	THE DREAM MERCHANTS	Harold Robbins	95p
T023 303	THE PIRATE	Harold Robbins	95p
T022 986	THE CARPETBAGGERS	Harold Robbins	£1.00
T027 503	WHERE LOVE HAS GONE	Harold Robbins	90p
T023 958	THE ADVENTURERS	Harold Robbins	£1.00
T025 241	THE INHERITORS	Harold Robbins	90p
T025 276	STILETTO	Harold Robbins	50p
T025 268	NEVER LEAVE ME	Harold Robbins	50p
T025 292	NEVER LOVE A STRANGER	Harold Robbins	90p
T022 226	A STONE FOR DANNY FISHER	Harold Robbins	80p
T025 284	79 PARK AVENUE	Harold Robbins	75p
T027 945	THE BETSY	Harold Robbins	90p
T029 557	RICH MAN, POOR MAN	Irwin Shaw	£1.10
T017 532	EVENING IN BYZANTIUM	Irwin Shaw	60p
T021 025	THE MAN	Irving Wallace	90p
T020 916	THE PRIZE	Irving Wallace	£1.00
T027 082	THE PLOT	Irving Wallace	£1.00
T030 253	THE THREE SIRENS	Irvin Wallace	£1.25

Historical

T022 196	KNIGHT WITH ARMOUR	Alfred Duggan	50p
T022 250	THE LADY FOR RANSOM	Alfred Duggan	50p
T017 958	FOUNDING FATHERS	Alfred Duggan	50p
T022 625	LEOPARDS AND LILIES	Alfred Duggan	60p
T023 079	LORD GEOFFREY'S FANCY	Alfred Duggan	60p
T024 903	THE KING OF ATHELNEY	Alfred Duggan	60p
T020 169	FOX 9: CUT AND THRUST	Adam Hardy	30p
T021 300	FOX 10: BOARDERS AWAY	Adam Hardy	35p
T023 125	FOX 11: FIRESHIP	Adam Hardy	35p
T024 946	FOX 12: BLOOD BEACH	Adam Hardy	35p

Science Fiction

T029 492	STRANGER IN A STRANGE LAND	Robert Heinlein	80p
T020 797	STAR BEAST	Robert Heinlein	35p
T029 484	I WILL FEAR NO EVIL	Robert Heinlein	95p
T026 817	THE HEAVEN MAKERS	Frank Herbert	35p
T027 279	DUNE	Frank Herbert	90p
T022 854	DUNE MESSIAH	Frank Herbert	60p
T023 974	THE GREEN BRAIN	Frank Herbert	35p
T012 859	QUEST FOR THE FUTURE	A. E. Van Vogt	35p
T015 270	THE WEAPON MAKERS	A. E. Van Vogt	30p
T023 265	EMPIRE OF THE ATOM	A. E. Van Vogt	40p
T027 473	THE FAR OUT WORLD OF A. E. VAN VOGT		
		A. E. Van Vogt	50p

War

T027 066	COLDITZ: THE GERMAN STORY	*Reinhold Eggers*	50p
T020 827	COLDITZ RECAPTURED	*Reinhold Eggers*	50p
T020 584	THE GOOD SHEPHERD	*C. S. Forester*	40p
T012 999	PQ 17 – CONVOY TO HELL	*Lund & Ludlam*	30p
T026 299	TRAWLERS GO TO WAR	*Lund & Ludlam*	50p
T025 438	LILLIPUT FLEET	*A. Cecil Hampshire*	50p
T020 495	ILLUSTRIOUS	*Kenneth Poolman*	40p
T018 032	ARK ROYAL	*Kenneth Poolman*	40p
T027 198	THE GREEN BERET	*Hilary St George Saunders*	50p
T027 171	THE RED BERET	*Hilary St George Saunders*	50p

Western

T017 893	EDGE 12: THE BIGGEST BOUNTY	*George Gilman*	30p
T023 931	EDGE 13: A TOWN CALLED HATE	*George Gilman*	35p
T020 002	EDGE 14: THE BIG GOLD	*George Gilman*	30p
T020 754	EDGE 15: BLOOD RUN	*George Gilman*	35p
T022 706	EDGE 16: THE FINAL SHOT	*George Gilman*	35p
T024 881	EDGE 17: VENGEANCE VALLEY	*George Gilman*	40p
T026 604	EDGE 18: TEN TOMBSTONES TO TEXAS	*George Gillman*	40p
T028 135	EDGE 19: ASHES AND DUST	*George Gillman*	40p

General

T017 400	CHOPPER	*Peter Cave*	30p
T022 838	MAMA	*Peter Cave*	35p
T021 009	SEX MANNERS FOR MEN	*Robert Chartham*	35p
T019 403	SEX MANNERS FOR ADVANCED LOVERS	*Robert Chartham*	30p
T023 206	THE BOOK OF LOVE	*Dr David Delvin*	90p

Mad

S006 739	MADVERTISING	70p
S006 292	MORE SNAPPY ANSWERS TO STUPID QUESTIONS	70p
S006 245	VOODOO MAD	70p
S006 741	MAD POWER	70p
S006 291	HOPPING MAD	70p

NEL P.O BOX 11, FALMOUTH, TR10 9EN, CORNWALL.

For U.K.: Customers should include to cover postage, 18p for the first book plus 8p per copy for each additional book ordered up to a maximum charge of 66p.

For B.F.P.O. and Eire: Customers should include to cover postage, 18p for the first book plus 8p per copy for the next 6 and thereafter 3p per book.

For Overseas: Customers should include to cover postage, 20p for the first book plus 10p per copy for each additional book.

Name ....

Address..

....

....

Title ....
(MARCH)

Whilst every effort is made to maintain prices, new editions or printings may carry an increased price and the actual price of the edition supplied will apply.